Walter Johnson

The Anatriptic Art

A history of the art termed anatripsis by Hippocrates, tripsis by Galen,

frictio by Celsus, manipulation by Beveridge, and medical rubbing in

ordinary language, from the earliest times to the present day.

Walter Johnson

The Anatriptic Art
A history of the art termed anatripsis by Hippocrates, tripsis by Galen, frictio by Celsus, manipulation by Beveridge, and medical rubbing in ordinary language, from the earliest times to the present day.

ISBN/EAN: 9783337223328

Printed in Europe, USA, Canada, Australia, Japan

Cover: Foto ©Andreas Hilbeck / pixelio.de

More available books at **www.hansebooks.com**

THE ANATRIPTIC ART:

A History of the Art

TERMED ANATRIPSIS BY HIPPOCRATES,
TRIPSIS BY GALEN, FRICTIO BY CELSUS,
MANIPULATION BY BEVERIDGE,

AND

MEDICAL RUBBING

IN ORDINARY LANGUAGE,

FROM THE EARLIEST TIMES TO THE PRESENT DAY.

FOLLOWED BY

AN ACCOUNT OF ITS VIRTUES IN THE CURE OF DISEASE
AND MAINTENANCE OF HEALTH,

With Illustrative Cases.

BY WALTER JOHNSON, M.B.

Πολλῶν ἔμπειρον δεῖ εἶναι τὸν ἰητρὸν, ἀτὰρ καὶ δὴ ἀνατρίψιος· ἀπὸ
γὰρ τοῦ αὐτέου ὀνόματος οὐ τωὐτὸ ἀποβαίνει.

HIPPOCRATES, Περι Αρθρων.
Littré, vol. iv. p. 100.

.

THE HEALER MUST BE A MAN EXPERIENCED IN MANY THINGS, AND ASSUREDLY IN
FRICTION ; FOR THE SAME EVENT FOLLOWS NOT THE SAME NAME.

LONDON:
SIMPKIN, MARSHALL & CO.
MDCCCLXVI.

PREFACE.

I AM very sensible of the numerous imperfections which disfigure this little essay. I could wish, among other things, that I had been more careful and more assiduous in recording the cases which I have treated frictionally during the past ten years. Instead of these few rough notes, I might then have presented to the profession a monograph deserving of its attention, and calculated to bring into better favour the simple, but valuable, remedy under notice. Cases of disease, if not minutely written down at the moment, can never be recalled *in detail* by the memory. Thus all that can be done now is to exhibit the great features of cases, and the grand results of treatment. Those cases which I have jotted down for publication are mostly typical, both as to the disease and as to the completeness of cure. I have treated many others,—some as successfully, and some with only partial effects. In some of these latter instances, the fault has been the impatience of the patient; in others, his want of opportunity or of pecuniary means; in still others, no doubt, my own imperfect skill was to blame.

The reader, in judging the sketch before him, will bear in mind the well-worn lines of Horace; and no one will receive it more gladly than myself, if any man bring into the light "*quid rectius istis.*"

WALTER JOHNSON.

GREAT MALVERN,
May 20*th*, 1866.

CHAPTER I.

THE HISTORY OF THE ART.

'Ιητρικῇ δὲ πάντα πάλαι ὑπάρχει, καὶ ἀρχὴ καὶ ὁδὸς εὑρημένη, καθ' ἣν καὶ τὰ εὑρημένα πολλά τε καὶ καλῶς ἔχοντα εὕρηται ἐν πολλῷ χρόνῳ, καὶ τὰ λοιπὰ εὑρεθήσεται, ἤν τις ἱκανός τε ἐὼν καὶ τὰ εὑρημένα εἰδὼς, ἐκ τουτέων ὁρμώμενος ζητέῃ. Ὅστις δὲ ταῦτα ἀποβαλὼν καὶ ἀποδοκιμάσας πάντα, ἑτέρῃ ὁδῷ καὶ ἑτέρῳ σχήματι ἐπιχειρέει ζητέειν καὶ φήσει τι εὑρηκέναι, ἐξηπάτηται καὶ ἐξαπατᾶται· ἀδύνατον γάρ.

HIPPOCRATES, περὶ Ἀρχαιῆς Ἰητρικῆς.

"But medicine hath of old both a principle and a discovered track whereby in a long time many and fine discoveries have been discovered, and the rest will be discovered, if any one who is both competent and knows what hath been discovered, start from these data on the search. But whoever, rejecting these, and despising all, shall undertake to search by a different track, and in a different manner, and shall say that he hath discovered something, will be deceived himself, and will deceive others; for it is impossible."

THE processes of Friction and Unction are broadly distinguished by Celsus, who states that the latter is advantageous in many cases in which the former is quite inadmissible. And this distinction is indeed useful for medical purposes, though it is true that there can be no unction (which is defined to be the rubbing in of greasy substances) without friction of some sort;

B

while friction was understood by ancient medical writers
to be usually performed by the aid of oil or fat.   Friction, therefore, might also be termed unction.   In the
operation of friction, however, the greasy substance is
used merely to keep the skin from chafing; but in
unction no more friction is employed than is necessary
to apply the oil.   Friction may be extremely gentle or
extremely rough—may be used for a few minutes, or
for hours continuously; but the friction employed in
unction is always gentle, and generally of short duration.   But as I said before, this is a medical distinction
—a distinction which naturally would very commonly
·be disregarded in ordinary language.

The practice of friction and unction, in other words
rubbing of the body with greasy substances, had its
origin in ante-historical ages, for the oldest writers
whose works are in our hands speak of the custom as
one in daily use.   It was employed sometimes as a
remedy, sometimes as a hygienic mean, sometimes as a
luxury, and sometimes it had a symbolic religious sense.
In the religious rite, the oil was usually *poured* over
the body, and for the most part over the head.   But it
is my intention here to disregard unction proper, in all
its applications, and to speak of that kind of unction
only which owes the main part of its virtue to the
accompanying friction.   Hippocrates, who flourished
in the time of the Peloponnesian war (which broke out
B.C. 431), frequently mentions friction as a recognised
and familiar remedy; and in one pregnant aphorism
he fully and tersely defines its effects.   Here and there
again he takes occasion to recommend friction in terms
which prove his practical acquaintance with its uses;—
as in the following passage, speaking of the treatment
of dislocation of the shoulder-joint after reduction, he

says:—" Those in whom the ligaments are attacked with inflammation cannot use the shoulder, for they are prevented by the pain and inflammatory tension. It is proper to treat such patients with cerate, and to bind the part with compresses and numerous bandages; to fill up the hollow of the armpit with a ball of soft cleansed wool, as a support for the bandage and a prop to the joint. To the arm there should be given for the most part an inclination upwards; for in this position the head of the shoulder will be most distinct from the spot into which it was dislocated. And when you have bandaged the shoulder, then it is proper to bind the arm to the side with a bandage passed round the body. *And it is necessary to rub the shoulder gently and smoothly. The physician must be experienced in many things, but assuredly also in rubbing; for things that have the same name have not the same effects. For rubbing can bind a joint which is too loose, and loosen a joint which is too hard. But I shall give a definition of rubbing in another discourse. However, a shoulder in the condition described should be rubbed with soft hands, and above all things gently; but the joint should be moved about, not violently, but so far as it can be done without producing pain.*"—HIPPOCRATES " Peri Arthrōn" Littré. Vol. iv., p. 100, et seq.

The writings of Plato abound with references, direct and indirect, to friction. A very remarkable passage occurs in the Menexenus. Socrates, in the course of a panegyric upon certain of his countrymen slain in battle, asserts that the first country which gave birth to men was Attica. And in proof of this view he adduces the fact that whatever brings forth offspring is provided by nature with food for that offspring. Now Attica, he says, is the native soil of wheat and barley, " by which the race of men is most excellently and best nourished."

" And after this," he says, " she caused to grow for her
children olive oil, the assuager of pain." Now here,
therefore, Plato, by the mouth of Socrates, reckons oil
as only less necessary to human life than wheat and
barley—not speaking of oil as an article of diet, but as
applied externally; because he terms it πόνων ἀρωγὴν,
"assuager of pain." And oil used in the way of friction
does allay pain in a remarkable manner; but taken
internally it has no such effect. The statements of
Plato are valuable not merely because they express the
opinion of a deep thinker, not merely because they
display to us one important element of the great
Hellenic system of personal hygiene, but also because
they reflect the doctrines of the medical school of Cos,
which in those days had already reached the summit of
its glory, and was without a rival in the world. The
chief of that school was Hippocrates, a man of tran-
scendent talent, who in later days received not unjustly
the title of Father of Medicine.

A passage occurs in Xenophon's account of the
Retreat of the Ten Thousand, which shows that it was
a habit of his soldiers daily to anoint themselves when
they had the opportunity. After sleeping one night in
the snow, says Xenophon, his soldiers were very loath
to rise when morning broke, because on shaking off the
snow they would feel the cold. But when the com-
mander himself rose, and, naked as he was, began to
cleave wood, the men were shamed out of their lethargy,
and rose up, lighted fires, and anointed themselves; for
much salve, which they used instead of oil, was found
there,—hogs' lard, and ointment of Sesamum, and
almonds, both the bitter and terebinthinate.

A few years later, we find Aristotle recommending
as a remedy against weariness, rubbing with oil and

water. (Prob. v. 6.) He also calls friction and warmth occasioned by gymnastic exercises, the "most liberal of the pleasures of touch." And we are told by Plutarch that Aristotle's pupil, Alexander, kept about his person one Athenophanes, whose business it was to rub the great conqueror, and to prepare his bath. Alexander's friends were not behind their master, for "they used fragrant ointment when they went to their inunction and bath," and they carried about with them rubbers, (triptai), and chamberlains.

Another incident in the life of Alexander is related by Plutarch, from which it appears that the Greek soothsayers gave to oil the same epithet as Plato, viz., "assuager of pain." The passage runs thus:—"For the chief of the bed-keepers, a Macedonian named Proxenos, while digging a place for the king's tent by the river Oxus, opened a well of oily and fatty fluid. But when the first portion had been drawn off, there immediately gushed forth pure and transparent oil, which seemed to differ from oil neither in smell nor taste, but was exactly like it in brilliancy and oiliness, and that, although the place bore no olive trees. Now the water of the Oxus itself is said to be extremely soft, so as to make the skin of those that bathe in it glisten. However, it was evident that Alexander was wonderfully cheered, from what he writes to Antipater, accounting this manifestation among the greatest that had been given him by the gods,—while the diviners held it to be a sign of a glorious but painful and difficult campaign; because oil was given by God to men to assuage their pains—ponōn arōgēn."

A. Cornelius Celsus, a very learned author, who wrote in the reign of Augustus or Tiberius, devotes a chapter of his work on Medicine to the consideration of the effects and uses of friction. He recommends it in a very great variety of cases, as I shall show by appropriate citations by-and-by.

Claudius Galenus, of Pergamus, practised medicine in Rome in the time of the Emperors Hadrianus and Marcus Antoninus. One of his voluminous writings is called, "On the Preservation of Health." And in this treatise he has discussed at great length the hygienic properties of rubbing, as will appear in an after part of this work. · Like Celsus, Galen recommends friction in an immense number of diseases—generally as auxiliary to other means.

But the Greeks and Romans were not the only members of the Aryan family who practised rubbing in the early ages. Strabo makes known to us the fact that the Indians, contemporary with Alexander, esteemed friction highly. "In the way of exercise," he says, "they think most highly of rubbing; and they polish their bodies smooth by ebony staves, and in other ways."—Strabo, xv., 709, cas.

Again, speaking of the manner in which their king received foreign ambassadors, he states:—"This is the rubbing with staves; for he listens and is rubbed at one and the same time. And there are four rubbers standing by."

How strange to find the same custom of rubbing still prevailing in India, that land of immutable tradition. In the "Private Life of an Eastern King," we read p. 188, "Let us take a glance at the Padshah Begum and her retinue, as she repairs to the holy Durgah to pray there. * * * * * * * * * A host of covered carriages of all kinds follow the eunuch, containing the ladies of the Padshah Begum's Court, * * * * the whole number of ladies so borne not being less than from a hundred and fifty to two hundred. You ask, What do they all do ? The answer is : They do all sorts of things. Some of them are professed story-tellers. * * * *Others shampoo well, and are so employed for hours every day.* Others," &c. &c. But it needs not the testimony of this writer to tell us, for all the world knows, that shampooing is an universal habit in India, and is almost as necessary to the native, rich or poor, as food.

If we consider the fact that in the time of Hippocrates rubbing with oil was spoken of as an old-established national habit among the Greeks, and also that the same practice was found universally prevalent in India by the chroniclers of Alexander's exploits in that country, we cannot fail, I think, to draw the inference that this custom existed among the common ancestors of both Greek and Hindoo. These were the Aryans, a noble people of central Asia, from whose loins issued Greek, and Roman, and Celt, and Teuton, and Persian, and Hindoo, and all their multiform posterity. And if we remember that in the days of Aryan greatness, The Bright Shining Air (Zeus) was not yet enthroned upon Olympus, neither was Power (Brahma) invested with the attributes of a Supreme Being, we shall be able to form some conception of the hoary antiquity of this art of rubbing.

Quitting for the present the classical writers of antiquity, I would draw attention to the good opinion which Lord Bacon entertained of rubbing. "Repair," he says, "is procured by nourishment; and nourishment is promoted four ways: 1st, by forwarding internal concoction, which drives forth the nourishment, as by medicines that invigorate the principal viscera; 2nd, by exciting the external parts to attract the nourishment,

as by exercise, *proper frictions, unctions*, and baths," &c.
&c.—"Advancement of Learning," book iv.

The first English physician who to my knowledge
made any considerable use of friction, is Dr. William
Balfour. A second edition of his book was published
in 1819.

In 1825, Mr. Cleobury published an account of the
"Rubbing System pursued by that eminent surgeon
Mr. Grosvenor, of Oxford."

The practice and writings, however, of these gentlemen failed to attract the attention of the profession,
and from that time to this, rubbing has been left
almost wholly in the hands of unprofessional persons;
some of whom, as Mr. Beveridge, of Edinburgh,
used simple rubbing, while others employed various
kinds of liniments and ointments, as the once
fashionable St. John Long, Mahomet of Brighton,
Harrup, and others. In 1859, Mr. John Beveridge,
son of Mr. Beveridge of Edinburgh, published a
pamphlet entitled "The Cure of Disease by Manipulation, commonly called Medical Rubbing." It is
written with much ability; and I shall have occasion
again to refer to it in an after part of this essay.

The ancients were unanimous in recommending friction as the elixir of age; and Lord Bacon, in his essay
on the art of prolonging life, bestows on it unsparing
praise. So, too, Dr. Réveillé Parise speaks of it with
approbation, although he was unacquainted with the
mode in which it is best administered. He says, "A
good, a wholesome custom of the ancients was that of
dry frictions over the whole surface of the body. And
this method has very marked advantages over the baths,
without having their inconveniences. The skin, that
vast organ for the depuration of the organism—that

great mean that nature unceasingly employs to maintain the temperature of the economy, to withdraw from the blood an excess of carbon, is wanting in functional energy in old age. Now dry frictions, more or less often repeated, are an excellent method of giving back to it a portion of its vitality. The aged will always derive great advantage from this hygienic measure; because its constant effect is to promote the circulation of the blood in the skin, to summon the fluids in larger quantity to the periphery; and thereby to maintain a higher temperature; to render the skin more elastic, more supple, more permeable; and so to augment cutaneous transpiration; to impress upon the cellular ganglionic tissues a secret movement of oscillation; and on the muscles themselves that degree of force, wherein results a general feeling of aptitude and comfort. It may be even that these frictions develope and favour in a sense favourable to health the electric power of the economy. But on this point we have only vague and uncertain ideas; because they refer to the insoluble problem of the elementary forces which rule the universe, and their relation with our economy. Be this as it may, the use of dry frictions over the surface of the body is an excellent mean to maintain health in old age. I have constantly seen that the small number of those who employ them are always well. An illustrious person of our time never fails to reply to all who complain of illness, 'It is because you do not rub yourself.' Among the ancients the fact was generally recognised that frictions with the strigil over the skin constituted a very appropriate mean of maintaining the strength."—Traité de la Vieillesse Hygiénique, Baillière; 1853. Mr. Urquhart, in a pamphlet on the Turkish bath, makes the following observations: "Who has not experienced in headaches and other pains relief from the most unartful rubbing? You receive a blow, and involuntarily rub the part. Cold will kill; the remedy is brandy and friction. The resources of this process surely deserve to be developed with as much care as that which has been bestowed upon the Materia Medica. Where practised, human suffering is relieved, obstructions are removed, indigestion is cured, paralysis and diseases of the spine, &c., arising from the loss of muscular power, are within its reach, while they are not under the control of our medicines. Here is a new method to add to the old. Wherever it can be employed, how much is it to be preferred to nauseating substances taken into the stomach! how much must the common practice of it tend to preserve the vitality of the whole frame! Even if disregarded as an enjoyment of health, it offers a solace which ought to be invaluable in the eye of a medical man, as of course it must be in that of the patient. We have all to play that part. Where the practice is familiar, it is used not merely in the bath, but upon all occasions. It is to be found without the bath, as among the Hindoos, some Tartar tribes, the Chinese, and the Sandwich Islanders. The latter present one of the most remarkable phenomena. The different ranks are of different stature. The chiefs are sunk in sloth and immorality; and yet it is not they, who, like the Grandees of Spain, are the diminutive and decrepit race. They are shampooed." Mr. Urquhart refers, in support of this assertion, to Sir George Simpson, who says: "But in addition to any or all of these possibilities one thing is certain,—that the easy and luxurious life of a chief has had very considerable influence in the matter. He or she, as the case may be, fares sumptuously every day, or rather every hour, and takes little or no exercise, while the constant habit of being shampooed after every regular meal, and oftener if desirable or expedient, promotes circulation or digestion without superinducing either exhaustion or fatigue."—"Voyage round the World." Vol. ii. p. 51.

I have now traced, very incompletely, in outline, the history of the venerable custom of rubbing; and will only add that in ancient, as in modern times, friction was considered very conducive to the health of animals. The horse, as every one knows, is much improved in condition by regular friction. In England this is accomplished by the curry-comb, or a wisp of straw, but in India, as in ancient Greece, the groom rubs his horse with his own naked hand. My Indian friends assure me that their horses have, in consequence, a far finer coat than English horses.

Friction is also useful to the dog. Arrian says, "And great is the advantage to the dog of rubbing of the whole body—not less than to the horse, for it is good to knit and strengthen the limbs, and it makes the hair soft, and its hue glossy, and it cleanses the impurities of the skin. One should rub the back and the loins with the right hand, placing the left hand under the belly, in order that the dog may not be hurt from being squeezed from above into a crouching position; and the ribs should be rubbed with both hands; and the buttocks as far as the extremities of the feet; and the shoulder blades as well. And when they seem to have had enough, lift her up by the tail, and having given her a stretching, let her go. And she will shake herself, when let go, and show that she liked the treatment."—"Arrian Cynegeticus." Ed. R. Hercher: Teubner.

CHAPTER II.

'Ανάτριψις δύναται λῦσαι, δῆσαι, σαρκῶσαι, μινυθῆσαι·
ἡ σκληρὴ δῆσαι· ἡ μαλακὴ λῦσαι· ἡ πολλὴ μινυθῆσαι· ἡ
μετρίη παχῦναι.——HIPPOCRATES.

"Rubbing can bind and loosen; can make flesh, and cause parts to
waste. Hard rubbing binds; soft rubbing loosens; much rubbing
causes parts to waste; moderate rubbing makes them grow."

THE rubbing practices of the Greeks and Romans
may be considered under two heads, viz., as simple
rubbing, and as rubbing in connection with the bath or
gymnastic exercises. Again, simple rubbing was either
local, and applied to the part affected; or local, and
applied to a distant part; or general. As an example
of local rubbing, applied to the part affected, we may
cite the case of inflammation of the ligaments of the
shoulder, consequent upon dislocation. In this accident,
Hippocrates advises the surgeon, after reduction, "to
rub the shoulder gently and smoothly." And Celsus
recommends, in consumptive cough, "stroking of the
chest with a gentle hand;" in vehement pain of the
head, produced by cold, "strong rubbing of the head;"
in cynic spasm, "soft and long-continued rubbing of
the affected part;" in paralysis of the tongue, "strongly
rub the head and mouth, and the parts beneath the
chin, and the neck." In catarrh, he tells us, after
taking brisk walking exercise under cover, "to rub the

head and mouth more than fifty times." In empros-
thotonos and opisthotonos, forms of tetanus or lock-jaw,
he recommends one "to rub the neck and shoulder-
blade with old oil." In cough from ulceration of the
throat, we are to have "the chest rubbed for a long
time." In excessive pain in the hips, "if there is no
ulceration, the friction must be applied to the hips
themselves."

This local rubbing seems to have been performed
with the palm of the hand, or with the under part of
the fingers held together. The object of this kind of
rubbing appears to be, first to draw out inflammation
from the interior to the exterior, as in the case of
inflammation of the ligaments, and cough and catarrh;
or, second, to disperse local deposits, as in "excessive
pain in the hips," by which, no doubt, Celsus means
what we now term sciatica; for he says expressly, in
treating of this disease, "One must use friction also,
particularly in the sun, and several times the same day,
*in order that the matters which by their collection have
produced the mischief, may be the more easily dispersed.*"
The second form of local friction is applied to parts
distant from the disease. Thus in inward suppurations,
Celsus states, "But it will be necessary to apply rubbing
to those parts which are not affected." In catarrh, in
asthma, in ulceration of the throat, in ulceration of the
stomach, in liver diseases, he advises strong friction of
the lower extremities. In "vomiting, and pain in the
stomach," in pleurisy, in peripneumonia, in ileus, in
flatulent colic of the cœcum, he recommends rubbing
of the arms and legs. In dropsy, he recommends
chiefly the upper extremities to be rubbed. The reason
for this prescription he gives thus:—"But far more
frequently, when one part is in pain, another part must

be rubbed, and particularly when we desire to draw matter from the upper or middle parts of the body, and therefore rub the extremities." This kind of rubbing, we may suppose, was effected by encircling the limb with the palm of the hand, and making up and down strokes with firm pressure, or sweeping the hand, as it were, round the limb.

General rubbing is extolled by Celsus in slow fevers without remission (with oil and salt); in chilliness before fevers (with warm oil and some warming substance); in tertian fever with complete intermissions; in quartan fever; in frenzy; in difficulty of sleeping in frenzied persons (extremely lightly); in melancholia; in extreme sadness in lunatics; in madness generally; in flatulence, and consequent pain, in dropsical persons (with oil and some warming substance); in leuco-phlegmatia (with soft hands moistened with salt and water, to which a little oil has been added); in atrophy; in cachexia; in phthisis (some warming substances should sometimes be added to the oil, to produce perspiration); in bad habit of body; in epilepsy (with *old* oil, which is more stimulating than new oil); in jaundice; in elephantiasis; in apoplexy; in old headaches; in moist cough from ulceration of the throat (with some warming substance); in flatulence; in paralysis of the stomach, and consequent wasting; in loading of the stomach with phlegm; in splenic disease; in the cœliac form of colic (with nitre and oil); in the lienteric form of diarrhœa; in hysterics; in unusual flow of urine; in thickness of urine; in spermatorrhœa; in gout; and in tardy convalescence.

The object which the old physicians sought to gain by this general rubbing in these cases was twofold. Firstly, they tried to draw out the internal fever to the surface; and Celsus remarks,—"A patient is in a bad state when the exterior of the body is cold, the interior hot with thirst. But indeed also the only safeguard lies in rubbing; but if it shall have called forth the heat into the skin, it may make room for some medicinal treatment." And this is evidently his reason for urging the use of rubbings in the inflammations of the brain, chest, and abdomen, before enumerated. The second object is thus stated:—"But rubbing should sometimes be applied to the whole body, as when an invalid requires his system to be replenished." And again,— "But when weakness of the body needs this cure over its whole extent, it ought to be shorter and more gentle (than local rubbing), so as only to soften the superficial skin; that it may be enabled the more easily to receive new matter from the food." The manner of rubbing in these cases is not stated, but we may infer that the palm of the hand was employed, from Celsus' expression, "the hands must be applied (manus dimovendæ) less frequently in the case of a woman than a man." So much for the therapeutic uses of rubbing among the ancients.

Now let us consider how they employed the same agent as a hygienic appliance.

The great schools of hygiene in classical times, but pre-eminently in the days of Grecian glory, were the Gymnasia. The gymnasium was in Athens and Sparta a State institution, and it was frequented by every free-born citizen. Solon watched over it with jealous care, and regulated by law even such apparently trifling matters as the hours of its opening and closing. So strict was he in maintaining the sacredness of its character, that he punished with death any slave detected within its precincts. We may from these facts under-

stand how essential this great lawgiver deemed the
physical education of his people, and how strong his
conviction was that this physical education was accomplished by the gymnasium. Now what were the
processes therein resorted to? They may be resolved
into three divisions, viz., exercises, frictions, baths.
The exercises comprised wrestling, boxing, running,
jumping, throwing the quoit and the spear, and the
game of ball. There were other exercises also, but
these were the important ones. Frictions with oil were
used to prepare the young men *before* their exercises, to
refresh them *after* their exercises, and after the bath.
The baths were, the hot-air sweating (the laconicum), the
warm or hot bath, and the cold bath, which, however,
was sometimes omitted; and to replace it the gymnasium was built on the banks of a river, in order that
the exercise of swimming might be conjoined with the
hardening action of the cold water. The usual routine
was this:—The youth was first rubbed by the paidotribes
with oil; this process was called the preparatory rubbing
—tripsis paraskeuastiké. He then proceeded to some
of the lighter exercises, as playing at ball; after which
he sprinkled himself with Egyptian dust, and sought a
companion (sungumnastes) to wrestle with. When
sufficiently exercised, he passed into the room of the
anointer (aleiptes), who by aid of the stlengis or strigil,
as the Romans called it, helped him to scrape off his
dust, oil, and sweat, and then rubbed him again with
oil, which process was called apotherapeia. This done,
he entered the warm bath, and after a short stay
proceeded to the cold bath, and from the cold bath he
returned to the aleiptes, who anointed him a second
time, and sent him about his business. It ought never
to be forgotten that the aleiptes regulated the diet of

every pupil, prescribing the exact quantity and quality
and time of every meal. It is not my intention to enter
into details on the subject of the gymnasium; but I am
compelled thus briefly to allude to it in order to render
intelligible what remains to be said about gymnastic
friction. Gymnastic or hygienic friction, then, consisted in the preparatory friction—tripsis paraskeuastiké,—and the friction which followed the exercises
—apotherapeia. The former is thus described by
Galen (Peri Hugeeinōn Logos, B.):—"Hence if
anyone, immediately after undressing, proceed to the
more violent movements before he has softened the
whole body, and thinned the excretions, and opened the
pores, he incurs the danger of breaking or spraining
some of the solid parts. There is danger also of the
excretions, in the rush of moving spirits, blocking up
the pores. But if beforehand you gradually warm and
soften the solids and thin the fluids, and expand the
pores, the person exercising will run no danger of
breaking any part, nor of blocking up the pores.
Hence, in order to insure this result, it is proper, by
moderate rubbing with a linen cloth, to warm the whole
body beforehand, and then to rub with oil. For I do
not counsel the immediate application of the grease
before the skin is warmed and the pores expanded, and,
generally speaking, before the body is prepared to
receive the oil; and this will be accomplished by a very
few turns of the hands, without pain and moderately
quick, having in view to warm the body without
compressing it; for you will perceive while this is being
done a blooming redness running over the whole skin;
and then is the time to apply the grease to it, and rub
with bare hands, observing a medium hardness and
softness, in order that the body may not be contracted

and compressed, nor loosened and relaxed beyond the
fitting extent, but be kept in its natural state. And
one should at first rub quietly, and afterwards gradually
increasing it, push the strength of the friction so far as
evidently to compress the flesh, but not to bruise it.
But it is not proper to apply such strong friction for a
long time, but once or twice to each part; for we do
not rub so as to harden the body of the boy, whom we
are now training for the exercises, but to excite it to
activity and augment its tone, and contract its porous-
ness; for it is proper to preserve his body in a medium
state, and by no means to make it hard or dry, lest we
should by chance check somewhat of the natural growth.
But in the process of time, when the youth is entering
upon manhood, then we shall ·use harder friction and
cold baths, after the gymnastic exercises; but of this
we will speak again. In using friction preparatory to
the gymnastic exercises, the use of which is to soften
the body, the middle quality between hard and soft
should prevail, and all else should take its fashion
accordingly. And in the imposition and circumflexion
of the hands the rubbing should be very varied, and not
merely directed from above to below, nor from below to
above, but also slanting and oblique, transverse and
sub-transverse. I term transverse that which is the
opposite to perpendicular, and sub-transverse that which
deviates a little from the transverse on either side; just
as I term slanting that which turns on either side of
the perpendicular; but the direction exactly between
the perpendicular and the transverse I term oblique;
and it will make no difference whether you use the
expression, tripsis (rubbing), or anatripsis (rubbing up,
or as we should say, rubbing down), seeing that the
latter is more usual among the ancients and the former

among the moderns. And I recommend the imposition and circumflexion of the hands to be varied, in order that all the fibres of the muscles, as completely as possible, in every part, may be rubbed: for the opinion that transverse rubbing, which some call circular rubbing, hardens and condenses, and contracts and binds the body, but that perpendicular rubbing rarifies and dilates, and softens and unbinds, is a mark of the same ignorance from which proceed most of the other assertions made by gymnastic professors on the subject of rubbing."

Immediately after these paragraphs follows a long and prolix refutation of certain statements put forth by one Theon, who, having been an athlete, became professor of gymnastics, and head of a school in Alexandria. In a book on this subject, Theon put forward an imaginary emendation of the celebrated aphorism of Hippocrates concerning rubbing. Galen is indignant that any man, and particularly one not brought up to medicine from his youth, should consider his own knowledge of rubbing to be superior to that of the Great Master; hence in many pages a refutation of Theon's fallacies. After this digression, Galen recurs to the subject of the tripsis paraskeuastiké, and then he passes on to the apotherapeia. I give his words:—" Rubbing which prepares for gymnastic exercises, and that which follows the same, is subservient to the exercises. The former heats and moderately opens the pores, and liquifies the excretions retained in the flesh, and softens the solid parts, and this is termed preparatory or paraskeuastic rubbing. But the other is termed after-ministering (apotherapeutic); and as it is applied with a larger amount of oil, it at the same time moistens by means of the grease, and softens the solid parts, and carries off what is contained in the pores; but of this we shall speak again after we have treated of the gymnastic exercises. Now the preparatory rubbing received by a person of the best constitution of body for the sake of warming ought to be applied a little before,—soft at first, but as they are about to commence the exercises, hard. For, used after this plan, it will be best able to soften, and excite to freedom of action, and to maintain the condition of the body such as it received it. If, however, any mistake is to be made, let it be on the side of hardness; for a few excesses beyond moderation stop at the skin, and effect no change in the internal parts; and no injury is produced if the skin is rendered a little too hard and thick, for thereby its sensibility would be diminished, so that if transpiration could readily go on through a skin in this condition, it would be our object to make it very hard and thick. But now, since it has to be properly prepared for both objects, viz., for the transpiration of the excretions from within, and against the force of impact from without, the mean between both excesses will be best; but if, indeed, this should not be observed, the harder and thicker state is better than the softer and more rare; for the defect of transpiration it is possible to rectify by the gymnastic exercises; but for the fault of the other state, viz., the readiness to sustain injury from external causes, there is no other rectification at hand; and no slight harm attends upon it, inasmuch as frequently not only the excretions are carried off, but also the food itself. Certainly, as respects the difference of quality, it is better to err on the side of hardness than of softness; but as respects quantity, on the side of brevity—that is to say, in the case of a constitution and age such as we are treating of; for we must always remember this in the present discussion, that we are desirous of still promoting growth, and by no means of drying up. But what constitutions of body, according to their affections, we must rub more, I shall explain by-and-bye."

Galen next refers to the length of time which it is proper to continue the rubbing at one application. This he says must depend upon other considerations, such as the temperature of the surrounding air, as determined by season, locality, &c. And then he goes on to remark, "These are the signs of moderate rubbing, in a medium state of the atmosphere, and a healthy condition of body, *Redness* and *Swelling*. For, as in the affusion of warm water, at first the body enlarges, but if the affusion is continued, contracts; wherefore Hippocrates said, 'At first the body is increased, but afterwards diminished in bulk;" so also rubbing at first increases it in bulk, but afterwards contracts and purges the body. Those, therefore, who are rubbed with a view of gaining flesh, ought then to leave off when the body is on the point of undergoing contraction. But those who are being prepared for the gymnastic exercises ought not to wait for this period, but stop long before, and, most of all, when they are in perfect health, and not advanced in age beyond childhood, for their bodies are moist and soft, and softened by brief rubbing. But the aim and end of preparatory rubbing is to soften the hard parts, to set free the fluids, and open the pores. But what shall be the duration of the rubbing it is impossible to declare in words; but the director, being experienced in these matters, on the first day must form a conjecture, which shall not be very accurate; but the next day, having already acquired some experience in the constitution of this subject, he will reduce his conjecture continually to greater accuracy."

Our author now takes up the subject of gymnastic exercises, and, having fully examined the kind and amount proper to be employed, reverts to the apotherapeia—that is to say, the rubbing of the body—which he asserts ought always to follow the exercises. "Its aim," he says, "is double, viz., to empty the excretions, and to preserve the body from fatigue. Now the former aim is common to every kind of gymnastic exertion, whether incurred by athletes or by any one performing any kind of necessary labour in daily life, as by those who dig. For we asserted that the objects of this also are in all two, viz., to strengthen the solid parts of the animal, and to empty the excretions. But the proper aim of apotherapeia is to check and prevent the fatigue which usually supervenes upon immoderate exertion. Now in the case of athletes, and indeed of those who dig, or take pedestrian exertion, or row, or go through any such toil necessary in daily life, weary pains (kopoi) occur more readily unless one has recourse to apotherapeia. But in the case of the subject of the present discourse (viz., a person of the best constitution and in perfect health, and free from any servile obligations, so as to be able to devote his whole time to the preservation of his health), the occurrence of fatigue is rare. For as athletes, even, who toil most of all men, experience no fatigue in any other kind of exercise, except in those which they term the consummating exercises, so those persons who live a free life, and take exercise solely for the sake of health, will never have to undergo fatigue; because they never incur the necessity of following this kind of exercises. It is necessary, indeed, to athletes, in order to prepare their bodies for

the labours of the contests, which are sometimes
immoderate and prolonged through the whole day, to
undertake these consummating exercises, which they
name also, kataskeué. But to those who exercise
solely for the sake of health, it is neither necessary nor
in any way useful to undergo excessive labours; so
that there is no danger of their being seized with
fatigue. But yet they ought to apply apotherapeia to
their bodies, if not from expectation of fatigue, at least
in order to empty the excretions. And it affords an
additional security against fatigue. For if moderation
in exercises be as much as possible devoid of the danger
of generating fatigue, and the character of their exertion
be removed from violence, it is possible that in both
some little thing may escape the gymnast, which over-
looked, causes to the person exercised, if to no great
extent, yet some slight fatigue. And it is not fitting
for one who lives for himself, and devotes his whole time
to the health of his body, to receive even the slightest
hurt. It is therefore safest always to have recourse to
the apotherapeia; but how it is to be applied, the
nature of the object in view will show. For since the
task is to effect an accurate evacuation of whatever
residue of the excretions, warmed and rendered thin by
the exercises, remain locked up in the solid parts of
the body of the animal, it is proper to undergo rubbing
by others—keeping the parts rubbed in a state of
tension; and besides this, what is called 'the holding
of the breath.' But since, like rubbing, holding of
the breath is not performed in one single way only, it
is better to select for both that kind which is most
useful. Now hard rubbing has been shown to possess
the property of binding,—that is, of making the body
denser and harder,—so that rubbing of this kind would

not be appropriate to the subject in hand; if indeed
that which is denser locks up within itself; but that
which is more relaxed allows the excretions to flow
through. And in the same way, to undergo a hardening
process, is most inimical to parts that are stretched (for
it increases their present disposition), but to be softened
is most advantageous to them. Since, therefore, it is
necessary at one and the same time to carry off the
excretions and soften the tense parts, we must avoid the
hard kinds of rubbing. And no less, I think, must we
shun slow rubbing, for since the body is no longer
moved of itself, there is danger of its being chilled and
made denser, receiving from without no warming
assistance. On this account, therefore, we must rub
not only inclining to swiftness, but with many hands
as far as possible, so that no part of the body may be
uncovered. But since the rubbing must be neither slow
nor hard, we must pour oil plentifully over the body of
the person who is rubbed; for this contributes both to
the quickness and softness of the rubbing; and it enjoys
also another very great advantage, for it relaxes tension
and softens the parts which have suffered in the more
violent kinds of exertion. For this reason we must
avoid hard rubbing; but for other reasons we must
avoid too soft rubbing also; for rubbing of this sort
penetrates to no depth, but its effect is exhausted on
the skin and parts near, and does not squeeze out the
excretions contained in the narrow portions of the
pores; for which reason, indeed, we advise tension of
the parts rubbed, and holding of the breath. Now the
mean between soft and hard, which is also moderate,
seems to avoid the inefficiency of the soft, and the
violence and hurtfulness of the hard. And it will be
accomplished, if the hands of the rubber be strongly

imposed, so that their pressure approach near to hardness, but from the quantity of oil and the quickness of their movement, fall so much short of it as to be accurately moderate; for the grease is no slight protection against the powerful pressure of the hands, and shortness of contact takes away from the power as from the time. And we enjoin, in the mean time, tension of the parts rubbed, in order that the whole of the excretions between the skin and the subjacent flesh may be evacuated through the skin; for if both be relaxed, it will come to pass that no more of the excretions will be forced outwards than inwards; but if the parts subjacent to the skin be tense, everything will be excreted outwardly, being compressed, as it were, by two hands—the one, the hands of the rubber externally applied; and for the very same reason the constraint and holding of the breath will be no small part of the apotherapeia. And it is named thus, when by contracting and drawing tight all the muscles of the chest which are about the ribs, we restrain expiration. For it comes to pass under these circumstances that the breath, while pressed by the sides, is prevented from being expired, on account of the closure of the larynx, but is pushed, the whole of it, below towards the diaphragm. At the same moment, the liver and spleen, and stomach, and some others which lie below, are all elevated toward the diaphragm. And it is necessary at the same time to contract quietly the muscles of the abdomen, in order that the parts which lie between, being compressed at the same time by them and by the diaphragm, as it were by two hands, may push out the excretions (perittōma) contained in them. Now the parts which lie between are the liver and spleen, and the stomach, and the prominent portions of the colon, and small intestines. And the places prepared for the reception of the expressed excretions are the whole broad space of the belly, and the cavities of the intestines therein situated. But if you leave the muscles of the abdomen wholly inactive, you will evacuate the excretions of some of these, but those of the chest and lungs you will transfer downwards. But it is better for them to be driven below, rather than remain in the latter, inasmuch as the evacuation of the contents of the abdomen is readier than that of the contents of the chest and lungs; for the former are vomited and ejected with ease, but the latter are cast out with effort, and force, and cough. But if any one, equally with the diaphragm, contract the abdominal muscles when holding his breath, the organs below the diaphragm will be more accurately purged, but he will transfer nothing from the organs of respiration to those of the food; but all their secretions will remain in the chest and lungs. Therefore, in truth I am unable to commend this kind of holding of the breath, and still less when a person not altogether contracting the diaphragm, draws the muscles of the abdomen strongly and forcibly tight. For in this case the vessels and parts of the neck must needs be filled with blood and spirits,—[*The vital spirits were supposed to be a thin kind of air, which permeated the whole body; their existence is denied by modern physiology,*]—and the excretions be borne upwards and towards the head, and not downwards into the abdomen. For we may see the same thing in flute players, and in those who speak very loudly or shrilly; for their whole neck is expanded, and their forehead swells, and the head is violently filled, because in this action the muscles of the abdomen are contracted, and the diaphragm yields to them.

But the whole of this action, as I have shown in my disquisition on the voice, is mixed and compounded of the greatest expiration and holding of the breath, and that in suddenly completed expiration the greatest amount of expiration occurs, consequent upon most violent contraction of the muscles of the chest and abdomen; but that in holding the breath the same contraction occurs in both sets of muscles, but no air is expired; but that in flute-players, and persons who speak shrilly, the muscles are contracted in the same manner, but the expiration is neither wholly checked nor completed all at once, but has a middle condition; so that to the three actions the tension of the muscles is common; but in suddenly completed expirations the rapid outward rush of the breath is peculiar; but in holding the breath, its retention; but in flute-players, and in speaking, moderate evacuation. And the larynx is the cause of these three actions, being open to the widest extent in suddenly completed expirations, but exactly closed in those who hold their breath; but having a middle state in those who play on the flute, and those who speak at once shrilly and loudly. On this subject, however, I shall have to speak again in my disquisition on Declamation. But that which is serviceable in the apotherapeia raises the abdomen, all the muscles of the chest being contracted, but those of the abdomen and diaphragm remaining relaxed; for by these means the excretions will be carried downwards. But the second rank is held by that which moderately contracts the muscles of the abdomen, in order that the organs below the diaphragm may receive the benefit of the apotherapeia. And with the same object in view, I would have executed the turnings of the bands which the rubbers perform round the whole abdomen, standing behind the person rubbed.   Others they perform standing in front, engirdling the back with cloths, which with their hands they draw about in various directions. And others they apply to the sides, and the spine, and the sternum, while the person rubbed keeps in a manner turning with them.   And similar applications and drawing round of the bands should be made over the loins, the person rubbed all the while throwing different parts of his body into a state of tenison to meet all of these, but not turning about to all, for he ought not to make continual or violent movements in the apotherapeia, but to make some, and at intervals to be rubbed; for continuous and violent rubbings are peculiar to the 'consummating   exercises.'   But   those   which   are neither continuous nor violent are proper to the apotherapeia; so that he should twist himself about, and often push back.   And at this season let him often change the person with whom he is engaged in exercise, and frequently placing himself behind, let him in turn entwine each of his legs about the gymnast, with no very great strain, while others opportunely lay hold of him and rub him.   For in this way he will best preserve the warmth of his body raised by the exercises, and will at the same time excrete, by his own straining and movements, the excretions; to which result the holding of the breath seems to me to contribute in no small degree, for pushed as it must be from all sides, it is compelled to descend into the small pores, and if it be pressed and pushed yet farther, it traverses them and bears with it something of the extenuated excretions."

The reader will perceive that the processes of the apotherapeia bear considerable resemblance to the shampooing of the Turks,—a circumstance not at all surprising when we remember that the so-called

Turkish Bath is only a mutilation of the Greek gymnasium, which the rude invader found existing as a time-hallowed institution, when he descended, scimetar in hand, upon polite Constantinople. No doubt the apotherapeia varied very greatly; for under the cunning hand of the gymnast passed the tender bodies of children, and luxurious patricians, the hardy soldier, and the stalwart, terrible athlete. Every rank in life, and both sexes, frequented the gymnasium, and therefore, without doubt, that subtile tact which distinguished the Græco-Roman civilization knew how to adapt its gymnastic training to these varied requirements. But the Turk, in adopting the Byzantian bath, threw away its accessories, its refinements, its elegancies, its nice distinctions and graduations; and retained only its most essential elements. Hence, I suppose, the coarseness of the Turkish bath. It is true that one must abate something from the description which travellers give; for, since in Turkey women go to the Bath, it cannot be possible that *their* limbs are wrenched and squeezed, and *their* bodies trampled upon, as we are told is the case with the men. At least for the upper classes the operations must be more delicate than we read of. Let the reader draw his own conclusion, after perusing the account which Mr. Urquhart gives of an Hammam in Constantinople:—"Under the dome there is an extensive platform of marble slabs; on this you get up; the cloths are taken from your head and shoulders; one is spread for you to lie on, the other is rolled for your head. You lie down on your back. The tellack (two, if the operation is properly performed) kneels at your side, and bending over, gripes and presses your chest, arms, and legs, passing from part to part like a bird shifting its place on a perch. He brings his whole weight on you with a jerk; follows the line of muscle with an anatomical thumb (percurrit agili corpus arte tractatrix manumque doctam spargit omnibus membris, Mart. iii., 82), draws the open hand strongly over the surface, particularly round the shoulder, turning you half up in so doing; stands with his feet on the thighs and on the chest, and slips down the ribs; then up again three times; and lastly doubling your arms, one after the other, on the chest, pushes with both hands down, beginning at the elbow; and then putting an arm under the back, and applying his chest to your crossed elbows, rolls on you across till you crack. You are now turned on your face; and in addition to the operation above described, he works his elbow round the edges of your shoulder-blades, and with the heel, hard, the angle of the neck. He concludes by hauling the body half up by each arm successively, while he stands with one foot on the opposite thigh. You are then raised for a moment to a sitting posture, and a contortion given to the small of the back with the knee, and a jerk to the neck by the two hands holding the temples."—"The Turkish Bath," pp. 22, 23.

The mode of rubbing pursued so successfully at Oxford, under the care of Mr. Grosvenor, in affections of the limbs, has been described by Mr. Cleobury in the following words: "The female rubber (for Mr. Grosvenor always employed females) seated on a low stool, and taking the patient's limb in her lap (which position gave her command over it) so as to enable her to rub with both hands, proceeded to rub with extended hands; so that the friction should be performed principally with the palm of the hand, taking long strokes;

one hand ascending as the other descended, keeping both hands in motion the whole time; and occasionally applying a small quantity of fine hair powder to the palms of her hands to prevent the moisture from producing an abrasion of the skin. After the friction had been continued in this manner for half an hour, the limb, if contracted, was taken by the female rubber at the ankle, and in the slightest possible degree an attempt was made to extend it. The friction was at first continued for one hour daily (more or less as the case would admit), and gradually increased till the patient could bear it to be rubbed an hour at a time three times in the day, observing always to rub by the watch."

The method of friction applied by Dr. Balfour in his rheumatic cases does not appear to have differed materially from the above. It was rubbing with the palm of the hand.

The method of the well-known Brighton rubber Harrup, consisted in rubbing with the flat hand. But Mr. Harrup employed stimulating lotions and plasters in addition. There is, however, a manner of rubbing introduced, I believe, by Mr. Beveridge, of Edinburgh, which differs essentially from all the previously described methods. It may be termed finger-rubbing. In this process the tips only of the thumb and fingers are used. Its advantages are—1st., the small extent of surface covered by the point of a finger, and 2nd., the exquisite delicacy of sensation of the tips of the fingers, 3rd., the flexibility of the fingers. Now the first advantage, that of covering a very small space, is very great in many cases, as when the part to be rubbed is very sensitive, and cannot bear to be covered over a large surface. And where inflammation is present, if the contact were over a considerable extent, increase of inflammation would result. Again we very frequently desire to rub a very small spot or line of the body, as a single nerve or vein or minute deposit of morbid matter. The second property enables us to graduate the degree of pressure, which is a matter of extreme importance. The finger of a good rubber will descend upon an excited and painful nerve (as in cases of neuralgia or hysteria) as gently as dew upon the grass, but upon a torpid callosity as heavily as the hoof of an elephant. The third property, viz., flexibility, gives rapidity of motion, which is very desirable in cases where there is extreme tenderness, or liability to inflammation in the part rubbed; for the brevity of the period of contact diminishes the intensity of the impression, and its effect is more evanescent. Hence pain and inflammation do not ensue, as they would from flat hand rubbing. The fingers of a good work-man dart from spot to spot like flies upon the surface of a pool. They never stay long on the same place, but are here, there, and everywhere, now rubbing lightly, now pressing heavily, now coaxing an angry nerve, now digging into a refractory callosity. Anatomical knowledge is the basis of this method, not necessarily the knowledge derived from dissection, but certainly that which flows from experience and the genuine wish to do good. As an illustration of the usefulness of this finger-friction I may quote the case of a gentleman who complained of pain in his shoulder. I had his shoulder rubbed for seven days, but got no good result. I then carefully examined the shoulder, and found a very painful spot, which I could just cover with my forefinger. Finger-pressure several times repeated upon the spot removed every vestige of the affection.

Rubbing media are very various. In the common way people rub with the hand merely, but this is objectionable, because it frequently chafes the skin. The ancients used a great variety of applications, such as common cloths (Sindones), olive oil (which was the ordinary medium, and which Socrates called ponōn arogēn—the assuager of pain), other oils, oils mixed with various heating drugs (as ammoniacum, cardamoms, &c.), oil mixed with astringents (as rough wine), oil mixed with irritants (as salt, nitre, &c.). The wild tribes of Armenia, Xenophon tells us, used to smear their bodies with hogs' lard because their poverty supplied nothing better; and his own army was driven to use the same cheap material on one occasion at least. Priessnitz rubbed his patients with water; and this, he said, led him to invent the douche. One night after he had been all day employed in rubbing patients with his hands wetted with water, he seriously considered whether he could not lighten his irksome labour. Suddenly, he says, there jumped into his mind the image of a column of water which fell in a neighbouring wood. Water has hands: let water then use them. The douche, therefore, as regarded by its inventor, was a water-rubber. Mr. Grosvenor used hair powder. Old women everywhere use opodeldoc. Mr. Beveridge found after many trials that pure hogs' lard, free from salt, answers best; and this, or olive oil, I generally use in my own practice.

I think upon the whole that, for common purposes, pure hogs' lard is the best medium we can use. The late Mr. Dineford made a fortune by his horse-hair gloves, with which at one time everybody thought it necessary to curry his skin; but of late we have not heard much about them. I ought not to omit to remark that rubbing has always been an essential element of the water treatment. Rubbing with wet towels; the wet rubbing sheet; the dry rubbing sheet; local friction with wet hands, &c.; and the admirable results which follow their application in suitable cases, are known to every one who knows anything at all of the water treatment.

The Turkish name for Shampooer, viz., Tellak, is probably a corrupt and abbreviated form of the Latin, Tractator; the harsh combination of consonants "*tr*" being softened into the more flowing sound of *ter*, or *tel*. The affinity between *r* and *l* is such that in the Coptic alphabet one character is common to both.

CHAPTER III

THE best definition of the local effects of rubbing is that given by Hippocrates two thousand years ago :—
'Ανάτριψις δύναται λῦσαι, δῆσαι, σαρκῶσαι, μινυθῆσαι· ἡ σκληρὴ δῆσαι· ἡ μαλακὴ λῦσαι· ἡ πολλὴ μινυθῆσαι· ἡ μετρίη παχῦναι. Which is thus translated by Celsus:— "Frictione, si vehemens sit, durari corpus; si lenis, molliri; si multa, minui; si modica, impleri." In English it runs thus:—"Rubbing can loosen, bind, make fleshy, waste; when hard, it binds; when soft, it loosens; long continued, it wastes; moderate in amount, it makes flesh."

And this indeed is the whole truth in a nutshell. The words "hard" and "soft," "long-continued," and "moderate in amount," must not, however, be strained to signify any fixed degree or duration, for they are relative terms. What is hard to one person is soft to another, and what would be long in one case would be moderate in another. The degree of pressure, and the length of duration must be determined by the acumen of the practitioner, and not by any invariable rule. Practice and experience, therefore, and not reading nor hearing lectures, make a man a rubber, and enable him to superintend rubbing. The effects of rubbing are waste or growth, and binding or loosening of the part rubbed. Tumours and effusions waste; emaciated parts grow; contractions are loosened; loose joints, relaxed ligaments, flabby muscles, pendulous breasts or abdomen are bound by judicious rubbing. It is easy to explain physiologically these apparently opposite effects. If any portion of the body be rubbed moderately, and for a moderate length of time, the effects produced will be a reddening of the skin, a sensation of warmth and comfort, swelling, softening of the tissues, and in some cases a perceptible filling of the superficial veins, and a moisture arising from augmented local perspiration. These are the primary, the filling-out effects, in virtue of which friction is a derivative and an anodyne. Now in sprains, contusions, and dislocations, we usually observe phenomena very similar to the above—not the same, but similar effects; and therefore we may conclude, from the formula of Similia Similibus, (if we attach any weight to that formula), that friction would prove an excellent remedy in all such accidents; and the constant experience of mankind does indeed confirm this conclusion. But we may go farther than this, and explain *how* friction removes inflammation, particularly such as is produced by a local injury. The first stage of inflammation is evinced by redness, swelling, increased heat, and pain in a part. These symptoms result from the influx of an undue quantity of blood ("Ubi stimulus ibi fluxus"), which distends and distresses the part into which it rushes. If the inflammation be very moderate, the distended tissues, by their own elasticity, gradually squeeze the blood out again, and matters return to the status in quo ante. But if the inflammation be very active, the tissues are distended by the inflowing blood beyond their elasticity, and they have no power to contract and push the blood out again. The blood ceases to circulate;

it stagnates; and from that moment a series of morbid changes sets in, which leads to suppuration, to sloughing, to ulceration. But if friction be applied *before* the circulation has ceased, *before* the blood has stagnated, then the circulation is kept up artificially. The blood is gently pushed out of the inflamed part by the finger, which thus plays the part that capillary elasticity is no longer able to play. The red and white globules of the blood are kept in motion, and prevented from cohering, and the fibrine is not permitted to coagulate. In this way, vital activity is maintained mechanically, stagnation is obviated, until little by little the blood is coaxed out of the congested parts, and the swelling goes down, and the danger is over.

The first observable results of rubbing are redness of the skin, swelling, and warmth. Sometimes one, sometimes another of these comes first, but generally they come pretty much together. If a part be moderately rubbed for a moderate time every day, after some days, or perhaps weeks, the superficial veins will enlarge, and stand out like cords, such as are seen in the limbs of a high-bred horse. If the friction has been immoderate, the parts will gradually become smaller; but if moderate, they will gradually grow. Here, then, the warmth, redness, and swelling prove that a larger quantity of blood has been attracted to the spot, and the subsequent enlargement of the external veins shows that the blood circulates permanently in larger quantity.

This, of course, satisfactorily accounts for the growth of the natural flesh, which is formed out of blood. Bring blood into a part, whether by rubbing or by voluntary exercise, and it *must* grow. Witness the

singer's throat, the dancer's leg, and the blacksmith's
arm.   But why does a tumour not grow, but waste,
and at last perish, if we bring blood into it by rubbing?
The reason is this: It is rare to find a tumour quite
isolated from connexion with the living body.   The
tumour is usually traversed by bloodvessels belonging
to the body, and the tumour also pushes its roots in
among the surrounding living textures.   Now the
rubbing brings blood in fuller streams into the tumour,
and round and about the tumor; it envelopes it in
blood, and pushes blood into its every cranny and
through its every pore; thus this foreign mass is a great
deal more completely than before brought under the
operation of the function of the blood.   But an
important function of the blood is to dissolve and
absorb dead matter.   Every part of our framework
dies piecemeal; and, as it dies, it is liquified and
swallowed up, and carried away by the blood to the
outer gates of the city of life; whence it is disgorged
into the external world.   The blood is thought by
physiologists to owe its destructive property to the
oxygen which it imbibes in the lungs; and if so, the
explanation of the effect of friction in promoting
absorption of diseased parts is easy.   The rubber's
finger, as it glides over every part of the surface of
the morbid mass, squeezes its molecules asunder.   The
cohesion of the constituent particles of the substance
rubbed is diminished; from a close and horny or gristly
or even bony hardness, the tumour assumes a soft and
spongy state.   The surrounding vital fluids are absorbed
by it, ooze into and through it.   Thus it is in every
part brought into contact with the oxygen which the
vital fluids contain.   And the oxygen combines with
the molecules to which it is presented, and detaches them

from the main body of the morbid growth. And these molecules then, thus altered, fall into the surrounding blood-streams, and are carried away to the excreting organs,—to the skin, or to the kidneys, or to the liver, or to the bowels, that they may be cast out of the economy. The mechanical action of friction prepares the way for the chemical action of oxygen. Thus if a chemist wishes to dissolve a piece of chalk, he breaks it up, and grinds it to powder first, and then pours upon it, in its pulverised state, his acid solvent. Chemical action occurs between the ultimate particles of sub-stances. Oxygen cannot act upon a tumour nor upon a stone in a lump. The tumour and the stone must be, as it were, broken up, that each atom of the tumour, and each atom of the stone, may be presented to an atom of oxygen. The fact that chemical action is essentially molecular, proves the necessity of mechani-cally separating the parts of a morbid growth, that its whole structure may be intimately penetrated by oxygen—if, indeed, we desire chemically to destroy such growth. The separation of the parts rubbed is not *wholly* mechanical, however. Friction gene-rates heat. Every one knows that two dry pieces of wood may be rubbed together until they ignite. So when any animal tissue is rubbed, it becomes warm; and, becoming warm, it dilates—it expands, as all matter, living and dead, expands when heated. This effect of friction, it will be observed, is favourable to chemical action; for heat diminishes the cohesion of bodies; and it is the cohesion of the parts of a body that opposes any chemical action to which the body may be exposed.

Among the secondary effects of medical friction, bruising is not unfrequently noticed. This does not

by any means indicate the impropriety of the process.
If the friction be continued, the bruising will disappear.
A part which is easily bruised is soft and delicate.
Rubbing will harden it—make it less tender. I have
often seen a limb bruise on very light rubbing at the
commencement of treatment, while after a time it
became almost impossible to bruise the same limb
by the hardest rubbing that could be applied by
the hand.

Another result, frequently seen, is the appearance of
an eruption, usually a blush like that of scarlet fever.
But occasionally this eruption assumes a vesicular, and
more rarely still, a pustular form. These are usually
treated by water compresses. Like the bruising, such
eruptions disappear of themselves, if the rubbing be
persisted in. They are favourable signs, as they relieve
the underlying parts. The phenomenon is in fact a
metastasis, in the language of medicine,—the disease
is drawn out, as ordinary people say. These eruptions
greatly resemble the eruptions which characterise the
water treatment, and which go by the name of
hydropathic crises. Sometimes, again, friction will
produce a boil, or even a crop of boils, when the
patient's system is charged with this tendency; and
then much judgment is required in so regulating the
rubbing as to prevent the occurrence of boils to an
inconvenient extent. *A few small boils* often do great
good, but too many might weaken the patient's system.
An old gentleman whom I know was improperly
rubbed on the back of the neck by a bathman. An
immense boil was the result; it was attended with
diffuse inflammation, and accompanied by fever. Suppuration and sloughing ensued; and for many days
it was questionable whether death would not be the

consequence. It is very manifest that as "you cannot make a Mercury out of any log," so you ought not to let any one that will, rub a patient.

Rubbing produces first redness, warmth, and swelling; and if the part was painful before the rubbing was commenced, immediately that these effects appear, pain ceases. This is a very remarkable fact, and one that ought to be universally known. It is, I repeat, an unquestionable fact. I have observed it times out of number in my patients, and I have frequently experienced it in my own person. If the rubbing be prolonged, the superficial veins usually swell, but they subside again when the rubbing is discontinued. The above effects may be termed the physiological effects. After a certain number of rubbings, however, the pathological effects declare themselves, and various forms of eruption are thrown out. Bearing now in mind the above quoted physiological and pathological effects of rubbing, we are perfectly able to understand why the Roman physicians recommended rubbing in so many diseases, widely differing in name and nature. In what diseases, chronic or acute, do physicians in this reign of Victoria not advise blisters and mustard poultices? What ailment is not more or less relieved by counter-irritation and derivation? But friction is a counter-irritant; friction is a derivative; friction brings the blood into the external tissues; and friction draws the disease into the external parts. When Celsus says, "A patient is in a bad state when the exterior of the body is cold, the interior hot with thirst. But indeed also the only safeguard lies in rubbing; but if it shall have called forth the heat into the skin, it may make room for some medicinal treatment,"—it is evident that he is recommending friction as a derivative; and as a

derivative friction will render good service in almost
the whole catalogue of known diseases.

It has been explained that friction causes healthy
parts to grow.   Now the ancient physicians took
advantage of this property, and employed friction to
improve the nutrition of weakly and emaciated persons.
Celsus says:—"Rubbing should sometimes be applied
to the whole body, as when an invalid requires his
system to be replenished."   Nothing is more certain as
a matter of fact—nothing is more easily explained
physiologically than this nutritive value of friction.
It is true that some attribute the result to the oil or
lard used in the process, but this is an error, in part
at least; oil and lard will not cause *muscles* to grow,
but *friction* with oil or any other substance causes the
harmonious growth of every tissue and texture.

The utility of friction as a preparation to gymnastic
exercises, and subsequently to them, has been so well
explained by Galen, as quoted in the preceding chapter,
that nothing need here be said on that subject.

Rubbing has a very peculiar effect upon the nervous
system.   I have produced sleep by delicate, soothing
strokings of the upper part of the back, in a sleepless
patient; and every one who is rubbed appropriately
has a tendency to sleep.   But there is a way of
rubbing which irritates and excites the nerves; and
an unskilled rubber, rubbing in this manner, will do
frightful mischief.   A lady suffering from spinal
weakness came to Malvern for change of air.   Here
she was introduced to a female rubber, who professed
to be able to do great things for her spine.   The lady
wrote to her ordinary medical attendant, who resided in
a distant town, and received his permission to be rubbed.
So the rubbing took place, and was persevered in, in

spite of a continued increase of unfavourable symptoms, until at last the lady grew so ill that I was sent for. I found her suffering from acute congestion of the brain. Now this affection was produced entirely by the injudicious rubbing.

The late Mr. Beveridge, of Edinburgh, had a great reputation as a rubber, and a great practice. His son, who died a year or two back, published a pamphlet, in which he put forth the leading doctrines of his father, perhaps slightly modified by himself. This pamphlet is entitled, "The Cure of Disease by Manipulation; commonly called Medical Rubbing." By John Beveridge, Great Malvern. London: William White, 36, Bloomsbury Street, 1859.—The pamphlet contains no cases, but is almost entirely devoted to the theory of rubbing; and for that reason I notice it in this place. Mr. Beveridge says, "It has ever been a practised method of reducing sprains, to use gentle rubbing with lard or any other unctuous substance, gently increasing the pressure until it could be borne by the sufferer so hardly rubbed as to soften the hard swelling under the skin. The process is simple; the cause of the cure by this means will appear in the sequel. Some have more tact in reducing a sprain by this· method than others. My father had this very remarkably; so much so that many who knew him used to resort to him when they had got sprained, and many were the sprained ankles, wrists, knee-joints, &c., that he cured. He always took great pleasure in this work; and so much practice as he had soon rendered it with him an art, and so expert that I could get dozens to tell that they have come to my father with sprains severe enough to prevent their putting their foot to the ground, and after an hour's treatment walk home quite well. This was in cases only, however, when the sprain was newly received. In cases where the sprain was of older standing, more treatment was required. I can remember being instructed in this curative art when very young, and could with ease reduce severe sprains before I was twelve years of age. On my father's retiring from business, he devoted the whole of his time to the service of those who were suffering from sprains and the effect of sprains. His practice increased very rapidly, as the results of sprains proved to embrace a much larger source of evil consequences than could have been imagined. Hip-joint disease, spine disease in many forms, and nervous affections, arising from injured spine, and spinal affections, white swelling, and neuralgia, and rheumatic affections, are only a few of the evils arising from causes which, if not sprains, yet bear so sufficient analogy to sprains as to come under the same mode of. treatment for their cure." In this paragraph we have the key-note of Beveridge's system. He regarded chronic diseases as pretty generally ancient sprains. It is a view which will excite the derision of the schools; but it is very singular how ingeniously it explains many common facts. Mr. Beveridge says, (p. 6):—"I will only desire it be kept in mind that, besides the blood, there are other and nearly as important fluids necessary to the healthy condition of the body. I will only treat in this preliminary work of the serous, cartilaginous, and synovial fluids. Of the first of these, the serous fluid, I must treat very slightly indeed; as, to do anything like justice to the pathology of this one fluid, would require a very elaborate work indeed. Its nature is compound, con-sisting of liquified albumen and the serum of the blood. Every cavity of the body, all the bowels are moistened by it; it moistens the muscles where they play on one another; it is also a constituent in all the membranes, and assimilates with all the other systems of the body, having great affinity for all of them. One of its features is its coagulability. From its presence in every part of the body, it is liable through over-abundance, poverty of congestion, or other causes, to create disturbance in any or every part of the body. From its coagulable qualities, it is more frequently subject to derangement than the other two fluids at present treated of. It requires long practice, and a nice touch, to discover upon examination when this fluid has been the cause of disease or injury. When this serous fluid is wanting, the treatment must be very carefully administered, but when over-abundant, hardened, congealed, or confined through inflammatory causes, the effect of the muscular treatment (friction) is very soon apparent in a speedy cure. I have had cases where by softening the serous fluid at the source of the muscle, a whole limb has been relieved from pain and stiffness."

Again, at p. 9, we read:—"When a part of the body has long to be kept in one position, so that any of the joints are twisted, a deposit of this fluid (the cartilaginous) takes place, which, if not treated in time, hardens into the constituency (consistency?) of cartilage. In one case I had a young lady who had suffered from sprained ankle-joint, which unfortunately, before she came to me, had been treated by blistering, and had terminated in a stiff joint. It was of some years' standing when she came to me. I reduced the sprain, but found that between the bone in the foot, on the inside, that approximate to the ankle in bending the joint, and the ankle-bone, a deposit of this fluid had taken place; and, from being so long unable to move the joint, it had hardened so as to resemble bone. Fortunately, there are no nerves in this substance, so that the reduction of this cartilage to its fluid state was attained without pain, but not without very hard labour. This jelly, having a strong affinity to serum, is liable to coagulate the serum when it has so far hardened as to be a deposit or cartilage, and accumulate the serous fluid in such parts. The treatment of such cases comes more under the head of serous irregularities than cartilaginous, for the process resorted to here is simply pressure applied in such a way as to bring the serous fluid into its proper liquid state, and to remove any extraneous material remaining in it, or rather assist nature to do so; for it is an undoubted fact, which the manipulating treatment has brought to light, that when any of the fluids, from any cause, have got into a hardened condition, it is only necessary by muscular treatment (friction) to reduce them to their natural state, to ensure the dispersion or absorption of an accumulated deposit, or even of any foreign matter that may have lodged in such masses."

The author next refers to the synovial fluid, and says, p. 13,—" When over exuberant, which is sometimes the case, hip-joint disease is easily engendered. This most often occurs in early years. White swelling sometimes arises from over exuberance of this fluid; and sometimes the state of the body is such as to produce what seldom, but sometimes does occur, an over-tenacity, thickening, or more glutinous state of the synovia. And above all, one cause of many evils is in the exudation of this fluid, and in its affinity for the serous fluid; so that if from any cause an escape of

it takes place, the consequence is that the serous fluid, into which it escapes, before long amalgamates with it. Sometimes I have known a slight escape through a little over exertion at the shoulder-joint, uniting with the serous fluid, which abounds in every part of the body, so affect the muscles of the arm as to require softening from the elbow-joint to the shoulder. When this exudation takes place at the base of the skull, and a deposit takes place there, evil results must ensue. I have had patients come to me with little hope of ever getting relief from headaches, caused from what they termed a flow of blood to the head. Many who have so come have not only been relieved, but most of them since being treated have never had the smallest recurrence of their headaches, or an approach thereto."
* * * "There are many who suffer from headaches and fulness of blood on the brain, who might easily, and often very easily, have relief from the same by simply having this deposit removed from the muscles overlying the veins which return the blood from the head."

Mr. Beveridge next proceeds to make certain remarks unnecessary to quote here, and in concluding his pamphlet states that, "Spinal curvature is a disease curable in most cases by this treatment."

Mr. Beveridge's theory that a great many diseases are produced by fluids, which exude out of joint-cavities, is founded upon the observation of certain facts not generally known.

If any surgeon or physician who has not hitherto had his attention directed to this point, will manipulate the flesh of his patients, he will be surprised to find in how many cases he will detect thickenings, hardenings, and swellings in various parts. He will find the necks of nearly all his patients who have suffered for any length of time from head affections, swollen and indurated, with most probably enlarged absorbent glands in the neighbourhood. The neck and shoulders will frequently be tender to the touch, and the muscular and other fibres will be dry, and will crackle perhaps on pressure. He will notice a similar condition of the shoulders and upper part of the back in asthmatic patients particularly; and he will find the long muscles of the back very much disordered in many chronic diseases affecting the stomach, liver, kidneys, &c. The arms and legs will on examination present swellings, and hardenings, and thickenings, accompanied by swollen glands in a multitude of patients. Now these symptoms, which had not been noticed before Beveridge by the profession—that is to say, by the modern profession—Beveridge discovered. He found, too, that such swellings can be dispersed by friction; and he found also that, coincidentally with the removal of these deposits, as he called them, the patients' health usually improved, and sometimes chronic diseases vanished. It was very natural, therefore, that a man whose mind was so occupied with sprains, should connect the above deposits also with sprains, and should arrive at the conclusion that a large part of the diseases which vex humanity arise from this homely cause. Mr. Beveridge was probably too hasty in his generalisation, but we ought in fairness to admit that no better solution of the facts, which he observed, has been put forward, except in the writings of Greek and Roman physicians, with whom Mr. Beveridge was probably unacquainted. A young gentleman, son of a wealthy merchant, was for many years subject to epileptic fits. He was treated in vain by the most eminent physicians of London and Edinburgh. At last he was cured by Mr. Beveridge. Mr. Beveridge discovered a crop of deposits, rubbed them away, and the lad got well. I knew the young gentleman, and I knew his parents, and there is no doubt of the truth of the above statement. What *were* those deposits which Mr. Beveridge rubbed away? I observe them continually in my own patients, and I have them rubbed away—to the great benefit of the sufferers. But in many cases I do not know what their nature is; I do not think them for the most part in any way connected with sprains. Sometimes they are rheumatic, sometimes they are scrofulous, but very often they are neither. Certainly the external tissues of our bodies are liable to morbid changes which are very little noticed, and therefore very little understood. I believe, however, that Galen and the ancient physicians were right in considering these accumulations to be not unfrequently retained excretions (perittōma), obstructed perspiration, in fact; and this idea is favoured by the wonderful rapidity with which a swelling is sometimes rubbed away. I have repeatedly known a very considerable swelling disappear in the course of half an hour's or an hour's rubbing. In some instances, doubtless, Beveridge's deposits are simply local congestions,—stases, as it was once the fashion to call parts swollen and distended by an over-abundant influx of blood.

Yet another word before I conclude this discussion on the physiology and pathology of friction. In the "Dublin Quarterly Journal of Medical Science," for Feb., 1866, there is an article by F. C .Donders, M.D., Professor of Physiology and Ophthalmology in the University of Utrecht. In this article, page 244, the learned Professor remarks:—"And if by the friction

in the capillaries, the oxygen united to the blood
corpuscles may be made active (that is, be converted
into ozone), which I have long thought probable, we
shall," &c. &c.   A note on this passage continues the
subject thus:—"Experiments of Saintpierre, Polytech-
nisches Journal, b. 162, h. 3, May, 1864, which have
reached me while these sheets are passing through the
press, seem to prove that mechanical friction really
ozonises the oxygen of the atmospheric air."

If, then, the ingenious conjecture of Donders, confirmed as it is by the experiments of Saintpierre, be
correct, we must trace the effect of friction on the
animal body in this way.

The oxygen introduced into the system by respiration
is of itself relatively inactive, and unable to attack and
destroy the living textures among which it circulates in
the blood of the capillary vessels.   By friction against
the walls of those vessels, it is made active, acquires, as
it were, teeth to bite the tissues, and then it gets the
name of ozone.   But the *increased* friction set up by
the tractation of the rubber, may well be supposed to
impart to oxygen this energy in *increased* quantity, in
other words, to energise a *larger amount* of inactive
oxygen.

Consequently, the actions of destruction and repara-
tion are stimulated to augmented activity, as before
explained.

APPENDIX.

Celsus. Ed. Ritters & Albers.

Book II. Chap. 14.

ON RUBBING.

Asclepiades, in the volume which he entitled, " On Common Aids," has put down so much on the subject of rubbing (as though he was its discoverer), that although he has mentioned three things only, viz., rubbing, water, and carriage exercise, yet he has occupied the greatest part with rubbing.

But it is fitting neither to defraud modern men in those matters, which they have either found or rightly followed, and yet to render to their authors such things as have been put down by earlier writers. Now it cannot be doubted that Asclepiades has more broadly and clearly inculcated *when* and *how* we should use rubbing; but he has discovered nothing, which has not been embraced in few words by that most ancient author, Hippocrates, who said that, by rubbing, if it be vehement, the body is hardened; if gentle, softened; if it be prolonged, wasted; if moderate, filled. It follows, therefore, that we should use it when either a body which is flabby (hebes) has to be constringed; one which has grown hard has to be softened; or one which is injured in any part by plethora, requires absorbent means; or one which is wasted and weak requires to be nourished. But yet, if one should weigh more carefully these varieties (which indeed is no business of the physician), he will easily understand that they all depend upon one cause (property) which takes away—that which promotes absorption. For a thing becomes constricted when we take away that which, by its interposition, produced relaxation; and softened, when we remove that which caused its hardness; and filled, not by the rubbing, but by the food, which afterwards penetrates to the skin, which has been relaxed by a kind of digestion (or removal of a portion of its tissue). It is a cause of things different in manner. But there is a wide distinction between anointing and rubbing. For even in acute and recent diseases, the body ought to be anointed, and stroked with the hand; in the remission, however, and before food. But the use of rubbing is unsuitable in acute diseases, and in diseases which have not reached their height, unless sleep is sought by it, in cases of frenzy. But chronic maladies, maladies which have already abated of their first violence, love this remedy. I am aware that some say, every remedy is necessary in diseases which are on the increase, not when they are already being terminated by themselves. But this is not so. For although, if left to itself, it would come to an end, yet a disease may be more quickly removed by the application of a remedy; which is necessary, for two reasons—both that health may be restored as soon as possible, and that the disease which remains may not, even from a slight cause, be exasperated. A disease may be less severe than it was, and yet not on that account be extinguished; but certain remnants may be left, which the application of a remedy shakes off. But as rubbing is rightly applied, even *after* the cessation of an illness, so it must never be applied during the increment of a fever; but if possible, when the body shall have been wholly freed from it; but if not so, assuredly when it shall have remitted. But rubbing should sometimes be applied to the whole body, as when an invalid requires his system to be replenished; sometimes to parts, either because the weakness of the limb itself, or that of another part, requires it. For chronic pains of the head are relieved by rubbing of the head itself; and a paralysed limb is strengthened by being rubbed.

But far more frequently, when one part is in pain, another part must be rubbed, and particularly when we desire to draw matter from the upper or middle parts of the body, and therefore rub the extremities. And we should pay no attention to those who define numerically how often anyone is to be rubbed; for this must be gathered from the strength of the individual; and if he is very feeble, fifty times may be enough; if more robust, it may be requisite to rub two hundred times; and between both limits, according to the strength. Hence it happens that the hands must be applied (dimovendæ) less frequently in the case of a woman than a man; less frequently in the case of a child or old person than in that of a young man. Lastly, if certain limbs are rubbed, long and powerful rubbing is required, for the whole body cannot soon be weakened through a part. And it is required to digest (remove by absorption) as much matter as possible, whether we relieve the limb itself, or another through it. But where weakness of the body needs this cure over its whole extent, it ought to be shorter and more gentle, so as only to soften the superficial skin, that it may be enabled the

more easily to receive new matter from the food. I have
before shewn that a patient is in a bad state when the
exterior of the body is cold, the interior hot with thirst.
But indeed also the only safeguard lies in rubbing. But
if it shall have called forth the heat into the skin, it
may make room for some medicinal treatment.

In feeble persons—Lib. 1, p. 17.

Exercise should be followed sometimes by anointing,
either in the sun or before a fire; sometimes by the
bath, but in a room as lofty and light and spacious as
possible. Next it is a rule common to all, who after
undergoing fatigue are about to take food, to walk a
little, if there is no bath, and be anointed in a warm
spot, whether in the sun or before a fire, and sweat.

For febrile sweating—p. 83.

If one be harassed by sweating, the skin should be
hardened by nitre or salt, mixed with oil; and if the
malady is slight, the body should be anointed with oil;
if more severe, with rose ointment, or quince, or myrtle
oil, to which astringent wine has been added.

In slow fevers, without remission—p. 85.

In these also rubbing with oil and salt seems salutary.

Chilliness before fevers—p. 87.

These parts must be rubbed with hands smeared with
old oil, to which some warming substance has been
added. Some physicians are satisfied with one rubbing,
and any kind of oil.

Shivering before fevers which run a certain course.

If nevertheless shivering shall have broken out, pour in between the clothes themselves a large quantity of warm oil, to which in like manner some warming substance has been added, and apply rubbing as much as he can bear, and particularly to his hands and feet, and let him (the patient) hold his breath. Nor must we leave off, although there be shivering; for perseverance in a remedy often conquers the malady in the body. * * * And the last remedies after these are, moving about in a carriage, and rubbing.

Tertian fever, with complete intermissions—p. 90.

But if the disease be not shaken off in the first days, but become chronic, let the patient stay in bed on the day when he expects the fever, and be rubbed.

Quartan fever—pp. 90, 91.

On the seventh day, anticipate the cold stage by the bath. If the fever shall have returned, open the bowels. When the body has rested·after this, have the body strongly rubbed during unction, and in the same way let the patient take food and wine. The next two days, let him abstain, continuing the rubbing. On the tenth day, try the bath again; and if afterwards the fever has returned, let him be rubbed in the same way, &c. The shivering itself must be subdued by the means above described. Afterwards it will be proper to be anointed, and strongly rubbed; to take a considerable quantity (fortiter) of strong food; drink as much wine as you like. The next day, when the body shall have rested sufficiently, walk, take exercise, be anointed, strongly rubbed, &c. * * * In an illness of this

kind, the remedies are, oil, rubbing, exercise, food, wine.
* * * If feebleness ensue, going about in a carriage
takes the place of exercise. If he cannot bear even
this, yet rubbing must be applied.

Phrenesis, frenzy—p. 93.

When the fever shall have abated, we must use
rubbing—more sparingly, however, in those who are
too gay than in those who are too sad.

Difficulty of sleeping in frenzied persons—p. 94.

Asclepiades said that these medicines (narcotic drugs,
as opium, henbane, mandragora) are out of place,
because they often turn the affection to lethargy. But
he recommended that the patient should on the first
day abstain from food, drink, sleep; that in the evening,
water should be given him to drink; that afterwards
light rubbing should be applied—so light that the
rubber should not even lay on his hand strongly; then
on the next day, after the same measures had all been
repeated, in the evening broth and water should be
given, and rubbing applied again; for by these means
we should obtain the accession of sleep.

Another kind of madness—p. 95.

There is another kind of madness, which lasts a
longer period, because it commonly begins without
fever, but afterwards excites slight feverishness. It
consists in a sadness which black bile seems to produce.
In this, the loss of blood is useful. If anything
prevent this, abstinence is the first thing; the second is
purging by veratrum album, and vomiting; after both
of which, rubbing is to be applied twice a day.

Extreme sadness in lunatics—p. 96.

If there is extreme sadness, gentle but long-continued friction twice a day is of advantage.

Madness—p. 96.

These rules are general; that the insane ought to be strongly exercised, to use long-continued rubbing, &c.

Dropsy—p. 100.

Walk much; run somewhat; have chiefly the upper extremities rubbed, holding your breath in the mean time. * * * In a man who from a quartan fever had fallen into a dropsy, Asclepiades has related that he employed abstinence and rubbing for two days; but on the third day he gave the patient, now free from fever and water, food and wine.

Flatulence and consequent frequent pain, in dropsical persons.

Moreover, it is requisite three or four times a day to use strong rubbing with oil and some warming substances.

Leucophlegmatia (anasarca—superficial dropsy)—p. 102.

If it be more severe, veil the head, and use rubbing by the hands moistened in water, to which salt and water and a little oil has been added. The hands of boys or women should be employed, in order that their touch may be softer; and that, if the strength permits, should be done during a whole hour before noon; after noon, during half an hour.

Atrophy, cachexia, phthisis—p. 104.

Besides this, it is good to walk in places as little cold as possible, avoiding the sun—(Celsus wrote in Italy)—to take exercise with the hands. If he be somewhat weaker, he should be carried about, anointed, rubbed, if possible chiefly by himself, pretty often on the same day, both before and after food. And some warming substances should sometimes be added to the oil, to produce perspiration. And it is of service, when fasting, to take hold of and draw the skin in many parts to relax it, or by putting on a plaster and pulling it away occasionally, to do the same thing.

Bad habit of body—p. 104.

But if there be a bad habit of body, first have recourse to abstinence; then open the bowels; then gradually give food; add the employment of exercises, unctions, rubbings.

Consumption—p. 105.

But if fever has not yet commenced its inroad, or has already abated, we must fly to moderate exercises, and particularly walking, also to gentle rubbings.

Cough and feverishness in consumptive persons—p. 106.

Then the extremities must be strongly rubbed three or four times a day. The chest must be stroked with a gentle hand. After food, wait an hour, and rub the legs and arms. * * * When one has begun to be a little better, he ought to resume exercise, rubbing, food, and afterwards to rub himself, holding his breath the while.

Epilepsy—pp. 107, 8.

When he is risen in the morning, let his body, except the head and abdomen, be gently soothed by friction with old oil. Then let him walk as far as possible in a straight direction. After the walk, let him be strongly and for a long time rubbed in a warm place, and not less than two hundred times, unless he is weak. Then let a large quantity of cold water be poured over his head; let him take a little food, rest, again walk before night, be a second time strongly rubbed so that the head and abdomen be not touched, &c. * * * To remove it you must only use exercise, prolonged rubbing, and such food as I have above named.

Jaundice—p. 109.

During the whole time exercise and rubbing must be used.

Elephantiasis—p. 110.

Rubbing must be applied.

Apoplexy.

Then (after blood lettings, &c.) use rubbings.

Pain in paralysed nerves—p. 111.

Water is to be drunk twice a day. The body must be gently rubbed in bed for a tolerable length of time: afterwards, while the patient holds his breath. In exercise, the upper parts should be rather moved; the bath is to be seldom used; occasional change of air by travelling. If there be pain, the part itself is to be anointed with nitre in water, without oil. Then let it be wrapped up, and a coal gently burning and sulphur placed beneath, and so let it be fumigated.

Trembling of the nerves—p. 111.

Drink water, use sharp exercise, also exercises and rubbings, principally by yourself.

Suppurations in some inward parts—p. 112.

But it will be necessary to apply rubbing to those parts which are not affected.

Vehement pain in the head, produced by cold—p. 116.

If the head be injured by cold, it will be proper to pour upon it warm sea water, or at least salt water, or water in which laurel has been boiled. Then strongly rub the head, afterwards fill with warm oil, and cover with a garment.

Old headache—p. 117.

These are general rules in every old headache: to cause sneezing, to rub strongly the lower extremities. * * * These rules are common to old headaches and dropsy: let the patient take exercise, sweat, be strongly rubbed, and take such food and drink which chiefly excite a flow of urine.

Cynic spasms, (a form of tetanus)—p. 117.

If by these means (blood letting, &c.) it be not removed, you must have recourse to running; and rubbing, soft and long-continued, of the affected part— of the other parts for a shorter period, but powerful.

Paralysis of the tongue—p. 117.

Strongly rub the head and mouth, and the parts beneath the chin and neck.

Catarrh—p. 118.

When we perceive anything of this sort, we ought at once to abstain from the sun, the bath, wine, venus; but under these circumstances we may still use unction, and take our usual food. We must, however, use brisk walking exercise, but under cover; and after it, rub the head and mouth more than fifty times. And it seldom happens that the affection is not removed, if we restrict ourselves for two days, or certainly three. * * *
Therefore, if in a person who is usually harassed for a longer period, and more severely, by catarrh, there has occurred a greater mucous discharge from the nose or throat than I mentioned just now, on the first days he must at once walk a great deal, have his lower extremities strongly rubbed, apply gentler friction to the chest and head, &c.

Opisthotonos, emprosthotonos, tetanus—p. 120.

It is therefore of more utility first to smear the neck with liquid cerate; then to apply ox-bladders, or bags full of warm oil, or a warm poultice of meal, or round pepper bruised with figs. But it is most useful to foment with warm salt; and I have already shown how it might be done. When any of these measures have been employed, it is necessary to bring the invalid before a fire, or, if it be summer, into the sun; and rub the neck and shoulder-blades and spine with (what is best) old oil; if that be not at hand, with Syrian oil; if even this is not to be procured, with very old lard. *Friction, although useful to all the vertebræ in man, is peculiarly so to the vertebræ of the neck.* Therefore, this remedy, with the interposition of certain intervals, must be used day and night.

Asthma, difficult breathing—p. 123.

Whatever excites the flow of urine is advantageous; but nothing more so than slow walking, almost to fatigue; much rubbing, particularly of the lower parts, either in the sun or before a fire, both by oneself and others, even to perspiration.

Ulceration of the throat—p. 123.

The exercise also of walking is necessary. Strong friction is to be applied from the chest to the whole of the inferior parts.

Cough, from ulceration of the throat—p. 124.

It is necessary to drink hyssop every other day; to run, holding the breath, but by no means in the dust; and to read with a very loud voice, which at first is prevented by the cough, afterwards overcomes it; then to walk; afterwards to take manual exercise; and have the chest rubbed for a long time. * * * Besides these, if it is moist, strong frictions with some warming substances are serviceable, so that the dry head be also strongly rubbed.

Flatulence—p. 127.

Exercise is to be taken, at first gently, then more briskly, and particularly such exercise as moves the upper parts, which kind is most applicable in all faults of the stomach. After the exercise, one needs unction, rubbing; the bath also sometimes, but more seldom.

Ulceration of the stomach—p. 127.

Exercise; friction of the lower parts.

Paralysis of the stomach, and consequent wasting.

Reading aloud, and exercises of the upper parts are necessary, as also unction and frictions.

Stomach loaded with phlegm—p. 128.

Exercise; being carried about; sailing; rubbing, are useful.

Vomiting, and pain in the stomach—p. 128.

If there is at once vomiting and pain, lay on the stomach a piece of uncleansed wool, or a sponge, full of vinegar, or a cooling poultice. But the arms and the legs must be rubbed, not long but powerfully, and made warm.

Pleurisy.

In the meantime, it will not be wrong to rub the extremities with oil and sulphur.

*Peripneumonia—***p.** 131.

Use friction for a very long time over the shoulder-blades, next to these to the arms and feet and legs, gently opposite the lungs, and do it twice a day.

Liver disease—p. 132.

Rub the extremities.

Splenic disease—p. 133.

Unction, friction, and sweating are necessary.

Cholera—p. 135.

If the extreme parts of the body are cold, they are to be anointed with warm oil, to which a little wax has been added, and nourished with warm fomentations.

Cœliacus-colic—p. 136.

But in the process of time, it will be necessary to be carried about, and particularly to sail; to be rubbed three or four times a day, so that nitre be added to the oil.

Ileus-colic—p. 137.

Rub the arms and legs.

Flatulent colic of the cœcum—p. 137.

And at the same time, determine matter to the extreme parts—that is, the legs and arms—by friction.

Lientery, (a form of diarrhœa).

Exercises and frictions are necessary to this disease also.

Mucous diarrhœa—p. 141.

On the third day, go into the bath; be strongly rubbed over the whole body, except the abdomen.

Hysterics—p. 143.

During the fit, rub the thighs and ham. In the intermediate time, use daily friction of the whole body, but particularly of the abdomen and ham.

Diuresis—p. 144.

There is need of exercise and friction, particularly in the sun or before a fire.

Thickness of urine—p. 144.

If the urine is thick, both the exercise and friction should be stronger, the stay in the bath longer.

Spermatorrhœa.

In this affection, strong frictions, affusions of very cold water, swimming in water as cold as possible, cold food and drink, are salutary.

Excessive pain in the hips—p. 145.

One must use friction also, particularly in the sun, and several times the same day, in order that the matters, which by their collection have produced the mischief, may be the more easily dispersed; and, if there be no ulceration, the friction must be applied to the hips themselves; if there be ulceration, to other parts.

Gout in the hands and feet—p. 146.

But when the pain is bad, the patient should be carried about, then move himself by gentle walking; and if it be in the foot, for short periods, now sit, now walk. Then, before he takes food, be gently rubbed, without the bath, in a warm place; sweat; have very cold water poured over him; then take food of a middle quality, eating between while things that promote the flow of urine; and as often as he becomes too full, vomit. * * * P. 147,—When the pain and inflammation have abated, which happens within forty days, unless the patient has committed some fault, he must use moderate exercises, gentle unctions, so that the joints be rubbed with acopum. (The ointment termed acopum—from *a*, not, and *kopos*, fatigue—was of a healing nature. It was considered good against weariness. Its composition varied; one form contained flowers of the round bulrush, laurel berries, ammoniacum, cardamoms, myrrh, burnt brass, Illyrian iris,

F

wax, Alexandrian reed, the round bulrush, Jerusalem rose, wood of the balsam tree, lard, and iris ointment).

Tardy Convalescence.

But from whatever disease a person is recovering, if he makes slow progress, he ought to wake early in the morning; nevertheless, to stay in bed; about the third hour, gently soothe his body with oiled hands. Afterwards, walk for pleasure as much as is good, avoiding every troublesome business; then be carried about a long time; use much friction; often change place, air, food, &c.

"A full account of the system of Friction, as adopted and pursued with the greatest success in cases of contracted joints, and lameness from various causes, by the late eminent Surgeon, John Grosvenor, Esq., of Oxford. With observations on those cases to which it is most applicable. By William Cleobury, member of the Royal College of Surgeons, London, and one of the Surgeons of the Radcliffe Infirmary, Oxford. Third edition. Oxford: Munday and - Slatter. London: Messrs. Hurst, Robinson & Co., Cheapside. 1825."

This little work, containing 170 pages, printed in very large type, commences with a dedication, "To the afflicted with lameness, whether from contracted, rheumatic, or diseased joints," which dedication, after recommending the free use of friction in the above-enumerated cases, closes with the following words :— "And should you be a soldier or officer, who has received a wound or injury that has affected the muscles or joints of your body, I feel that I cannot close this address without observing to you in particular, that though a great length of time may have elapsed since you received your injury, and though you may have considered your case hopeless, yet such is my confidence in this remedy, that I am persuaded, many of you, by applying it with patience and perseverance, may yet be restored."

The dedication is followed by a preface, and the preface is followed by a memoir of Mr. Grosvenor.

"Mr. Grosvenor was the son of Stephen Grosvenor,

F 2

Gent., Sub-Treasurer of Christ Church, in the University of Oxford, by Sarah, daughter of — Tottie, Vicar of Eccleshal, and was descended from a long line of ancestors, for many years settled at Ongarsheath, in the parish of Ashley, Staffordshire, a younger branch of the family of that name which came over with the Conqueror, and of which the elder is ennobled in the person of Earl Grosvenor, of Eaton Hall, Cheshire.

"Mr. Grosvenor was educated under Mr. Russell, of Worcester, a gentleman of great eminence in his profession, and after walking the hospitals in London, at a very early period of life obtained the situation of House Surgeon to the Lock Hospital. From this place he moved, in the year 1768, to Oxford, upon the invitation of his uncle, Dr. Tottie, Canon of Christ Church (the author of the well-known Sermons, and of the admirable epitaph on Bishop Hough, in Worcester Cathedral), a person then of great influence, and under whose appointment Mr. Stephen Grosvenor had, by accepting an office of no great consideration, at Christ Church, endeavoured to retrieve the prodigality of his father and grandfather, by which the estates of the family had been entirely dilapidated. Soon after his settlement at Oxford, Mr. Grosvenor succeeded to the place of Anatomical Surgeon, on Dr. Lee's foundation, which recommended him to the friendship of Mr. Parsons, the Reader under that endowment, and the most popular physician ever known in Oxford, between whom and himself the greatest intimacy afterwards subsisted, and which introduced him also into full practice at Christ Church. In this situation he distinguished himself by extraordinary skill and knowledge, and occasionally in the absence of the Reader he lectured to the students on topics applicable to the dissection of the day. Mr. Grosvenor gradually obtained considerable reputation as a surgeon; and on the death of Sir Charles Nourse, he found himself in complete possession, not only of nearly all the business in the University and City, but of that also on every side within thirty miles of Oxford. At one period he might be said almost wholly to have lived on horseback. * * * In the latter period of his practice, Mr. Grosvenor rendered himself justly celebrated throughout the kingdom by the application of friction to lameness, or imperfection of motion arising from stiff or diseased joints. He had first used it with success in a complaint of his own, a morbid affection of the knee; and by degrees its efficacy was so acknowledged that he was visited by patients from the most distant parts, of the highest rank and respectability; among others, by Mr. Hey, the able surgeon of Leeds, whose life has been given to the public by Mr. Pearson, of Golden Square. Those who have benefited by the process recommended by him, and pursued under his own immediate superintendence, in cases of this sort, and from total inability have been restored to a free use of their limbs, are best able to attest his merits. * * * He was twice married; first to Anne, daughter of — Hough, Esq., of the East India Company's Service, and widow of John Parsons, M.D., Chemical Professor and Anatomical Reader in the University of Oxford; and secondly, to Charlotte, daughter of the late Charles Marsack, Esq., of Caversham Park, in the county of Oxford. He left no issue by either marriage. He died at Oxford in the 81st year of his age, on the 30th June, 1823."

Having thus detailed such of the incidents in the life of Mr. Grosvenor as he considered worthy of remembrance, Mr. Cleobury proceeds with his "Full Account," &c. &c. The "full account" opens with these observations:—"As the late eminent and lamented surgeon, Mr. Grosvenor (perhaps from feelings of delicacy, or some other motives best known to himself), has not published the result of his extensive and successful practice in cases of lameness, and having witnessed myself the great benefit derived from the system of friction which he adopted and pursued for a series of years, I feel it therefore almost a duty due to the public, to lay before them, in as concise a manner as possible, the plan which he pursued; and at the same time to point out those cases to which it appears his practice is most applicable.

" I shall first briefly state (as it may not be generally understood) the particular mode in which friction was applied by him. For this purpose, females were engaged, who supported themselves by this occupation. The female rubber, seated on a low stool, and taking the patient's limb in her lap (which position gave her command over it), so as to enable her to rub with both hands, proceeded to rub with extended hands, so that the friction should be performed principally with the palm of the hand; taking long strokes, one hand ascending as the other descended; keeping both hands in motion the whole time; and occasionally applying a small quantity of fine hair powder to the palms of her hands, to prevent the moisture from producing an erosion of the skin. After the friction had been continued in this manner for half an hour, the limb, if contracted, was taken by the female rubber at the ankle, and in the slightest possible degree an attempt was made to extend it. The friction was at first continued for one hour daily (more or less as the case would admit), and gradually increased till the patient could bear it to be rubbed an hour at a time three hours in the day, observing always to rub by the watch. After every period of rubbing was concluded, however unpleasant and distressing it was to his patients, he invariably obliged them to put the limb to the ground and make efforts to walk; and he has been known to urge his patients to walk, though in the attempt they have been ready to faint with the exertion. From these attempts, repeated after every rubbing, the genial warmth produced by the friction has enabled the patients to do something more towards walking daily; and innumerable instances have been known of persons *perfectly lame*, and using *crutches*, throwing them aside in a fortnight or three weeks, when the friction was suited to the *disorder*. Though I would observe on the other hand that cases of lameness which left *but little* hope for the sufferers, have been removed, by *continual use* of this method for a *year* or *two*, contrary to all expectation.

"The cases in which it is most serviceable are:— First,—Contractions of the joints, unattended with inflammatory symptoms, proceeding from colds, damp beds, or rheumatism, attended with languid circulation and thickening of the ligaments. Secondly,—In those cases where there is too great a secretion of the synovial fluid in the joints, particularly in the knee joint. Thirdly,—After wounds in ligamentous, tendinous, or muscular parts, where the function of the limb or part is impaired; but even here it should not be made use of till the inflammation and tenderness have entirely subsided. For example, officers or men who have received wounds in different campaigns, which wounds are situated in the muscular parts of the back, thigh, calf of the leg and knee joint, elbow, or other joints; provided all foreign substances have been extracted. Fourthly,—In cases of paralysis. Fifthly,—Those of chorea (St. Vitus' Dance), combined with attention to the system. Sixthly,—Violent strains of the joints, where the inflammatory symptoms have entirely subsided. Seventhly,—In incipient cases of white swelling, for which disease it is well known that bleeding, cupping, and blistering generally fail; and that setons and issues bring the limb more rapidly to the knife. This is almost the only remedy that has been found effectual; and it has frequently happened that joints absolutely condemned to the knife, and on the point of being amputated, have been saved, and their use restored, by this method. For my own part, I should hesitate to remove any limb which it was possible friction might be of service to, till it had been fairly applied. Lastly,—After fractures of the articulating extremities of joints; as when the bones are united, a stiffness generally succeeds. In all the various cases of dislocation of the joints, when the motion of the joint is left impaired, if the inflammation has entirely subsided. In most cases of fracture of either of the extremities, when a stiffness succeeds their complete union; after ruptures in tendinous or ligamentous parts, provided they are firmly united; in weakly or rickety children, when the circulation is languid. Indeed, friction will be found beneficial in most cases where the circulation is languid, if unattended by inflammation. In fact, I feel it but due to the great talent of my esteemed friend, to be concise in whatever relates to him, aware as I am that I can add nothing to his fame. The enumeration of cases would be superfluous, as persons who have been his patients, and received benefit from his judgment, are dispersed not only throughout this kingdom, but in different parts of the Continent."

The remainder of Mr. Cleobury's book is for the most part occupied with the enumeration of cases treated, with one exception, by himself. Of these, I extract the following, in a more or less condensed form :—

Fluid in Knee Joint.

A.

A young lady was rendered lame by a large collection of fluid in the cavity of the knee-joint. Several of the most eminent surgeons in the metropolis were consulted on this case, which was eventually completely cured by friction and exercise, unremittingly persevered in for a year and a half. This was a case under the immediate care of Mr. Grosvenor, and one in which he took great interest.

Injury to the Knee. Lameness.

B.

A gentleman of the University injured his knee three years since, which rendered him so extremely lame at intervals, that he was induced to consult me. The joint was increased in circumference, and there was a considerable accumulation of fluid in the bursa situated beneath the tendon of the extensor muscles. Pressure on the patella (knee-pan) occasioned a dull, aching pain. He did not possess the power of extending his joint, and the weakness of it frequently occasioned his falling to the ground on making an effort to walk. He was rubbed regularly for three hours daily for nearly three months, at the expiration of which period he could extend the joint without any assistance, and was so far recovered as to be enabled to take walks into the country without inconvenience.

Diseased Knee-joint.

c.

Elizabeth Flaxman, aged about 25, came into the Infirmary on the 21st April, 1824, with the intention of having her left thigh removed, on account of a disease of the knee-joint, which had existed nearly three years. She had no power over the limb, and could not walk with the assistance of crutches. The knee-joint was considerably swollen, and the head of the fibula was much larger than natural. The muscles of the leg and thigh were subject to cramp and spasm, whenever she attempted to move the limb. I dissuaded her from having the joint removed, as I thought it a very proper case for friction and exercise. The joint was accordingly rubbed for three hours daily, and she was directed to walk about the ward, assisted by a female on each side, to prevent her falling. She persisted in this plan for four months, at the expiration of which period she could walk without assistance, and was discharged.

Injury to Knee.

D.

A lady fell down in Drury Lane theatre, and severely injured her knee. She was confined to her room several days, and soon after returned to her residence in the country. About a month afterwards, I was consulted. There was a considerable quantity of fluid in the joint; the bones grated on moving them; and she complained of a dull, aching pain. I pointed out the absolute necessity of rest, and directed soothing applications to the joint. These were continued for several months; but no great advantage being obtained, except an abatement of pain, a blister was directed, after which the soothing system was continued. The case still continued tedious, as most joint cases are. I recommended another opinion to be taken. It was therefore drawn up, and submitted to Sir Astley Cooper, who confirmed the system hitherto pursued, and directed a continuance of it. The ung. antim. tart. (tartar emetic ointment) was next applied to the joint, and continued for several months; after which, various applications were made use of, as occasion required. The joint, on admeasurement, was an inch larger in circumference than the other; the bones still grated on moving them, and the muscles were shrunk considerably. After being confined to her bed nearly three years, she was enabled to take a journey to London, to Sir A. Cooper, who directed the extract of belladonna to be applied to the joint, and rest still to be persevered in. This plan was likewise continued for several months; at the expiration of which period *she had not the smallest power in the limb, and was accustomed to compare it to a log of wood.*

Finding that we gained no ground, and as the joint was tolerably free from pain, I next directed friction to be employed. At first the joint would not bear it longer than twenty minutes three times a day. At length it could be endured for three hours daily (an hour at each time), during which process the limb was frequently but cautiously moved. I then directed that an attempt to walk should be made, but with the assistance of crutches. After the friction had been continued about three months, there were evident symptoms of amendment. I next directed the crutches to be entirely thrown aside, and prevailed on the lady to endeavour to walk with the assistance of an arm on each side. This plan was persevered in for eight months, during which period her improvement was progressive, and she can now walk without assistance.

Upon the above case I have only one remark to make, viz., that if friction had been judiciously applied, at the commencement, and without vainly waiting for the subsidence of the inflammation in the joint, the lady might, in my opinion, have been cured very easily within a few weeks of her accident. The surgical axiom that "Every inflamed part requires perfect rest," understood too absolutely, was the cause of four years of pain and suffering to this unfortunate patient. I would not, however, be supposed to sanction for one moment in the case of an inflamed joint *such* rubbing as was practised by Mr. Grosvenor's female rubbers. The only rubbing admissible and required, is the Hippocratic anatripsis, or the delicate finger-friction of the late Mr. Beveridge.

DR. BALFOUR.

"Illustrations of the Power of Compression and Percussion in the cure of Rheumatism, Gout, and Debility of the Extremities; and in promoting Health and Longevity. By William Balfour, M.D., Author of 'Illustrations of the power of Emetic Tartar in the cure of Fever, Inflammation, and Asthma, and in preventing Phthisis and Apoplexy.' Second Edition. Edinburgh: Peter Hill and Company; London: Longman, Hurst, Rees, Orme, and Brown; 1819."

Percussion and compression only, as remedial agents, are named in the *title* of this work; but from its perusal we find that friction also was much employed by the author, and is highly praised by him. Nearly the whole of the physiological explanation of the modus operandi of percussion, put forward in the first few pages, applies equally well to friction; and therefore, as it is well and plainly written, my readers will probably feel an interest in hearing what Dr. Balfour has to say. The following remarks are extracted from the introduction to his book. I again remind the reader that every word applies with full force to rubbing, although Dr. Balfour had not rubbing in his mind when he penned the paragraph. "It is impossible that man in his present condition can enjoy health uninterruptedly. He is daily and necessarily exposed to innumerable causes, which tend to subvert that balance of function which constitutes the perfection of health. Passions and affections of the mind, sudden vicissitudes of temperature, irregularity in exercise, in eating and drinking, and a thousand other causes, conspire to sub-

vert the balance of the circulation; on the equability of
which all the other functions of the body depend.   To
preserve equability of the circulation, then, is to preserve
health; to restore it, when lost, is to cure disease.   If
the circulation was always equable, no person would
ever die of apoplexy, or of inflammation of the brain,
or of inflammation of the lungs, or indeed of any inflammation whatever; no person would ever be afflicted with
rheumatism, or with any complaint consisting in obstruc-
tion of the vessels of the part affected.   If equability of
circulation was preserved, no person would ever die of
disease.   Death would in all cases be natural; that is
to say, the machine would stand still without pain,
without struggle; and not till extreme old age, and
from mere exhaustion.

"These observations render it indisputable that the
physician who points out the best means of preserving
and restoring the equability of circulation, confers the
greatest benefit on society; for health and longevity
must ever be considered the greatest blessings of life.

"Moderate exercise or motion is perhaps the most
useful and necessary of all the means made use of for
the preservation of health.   Without it health can
neither be perfect nor of long duration.   For however
perfect in all its parts the human body may be, and
however wisely adapted every organ to its peculiar
function, still motion is necessary to the preservation of
that balance in which health consists.   Without motion
or muscular action, circulation could not go on.   There
is a perpetual tendency to inequality in the distribution
of the fluids, owing equally to internal as to external
causes.   The force of the heart is not sufficient to propel
the blood to every part of the body alike.   The distance
of the extreme parts, the elasticity of the blood-vessels

themselves, conspire with other causes to render the muscles necessary auxiliaries to the heart in the distribution of the blood. After sleeping or sitting motionless for any length of time, we instinctively yawn and stretch and writhe every muscle of the body. What is the intention of nature in this? Certainly to restore that equilibrium to the circulation which was lost during perfect rest. The same thing takes place in the commencement of fever. During the first stage the patient yawns and writhes incessantly in order to prevent that irregular distribution of the blood, which is the consequence of the irregular distribution of the nervous power. If in these circumstances the equilibrium of the nervous energy could be restored and preserved, there would be no reaction or hot stage. The disease would be cut short at once. Emetics, by the convulsive motion they occasion in the whole body, produce these effects in a great degree. Hence their good effects in the commencement of fever; and not entirely as physicians have vainly imagined, from the evacuation of morbid matters from the stomach.

" But if muscular action or motion is necessary to the preservation of health in every stage of life, what is to become of those who are rendered incapable of it by the approach of old age or the invasion of disease ? In these circumstances we must have recourse to means very different from those employed during the vigour of life and of health. In the latter case business, amusement, and that principle of action which is inherent in us, and which is observable from our earliest infancy, impel us to the quantum of exercise necessary to health; in the former case all these causes cease to operate, and we are compelled to inactivity. If a substitute can be found for walking and riding on horseback,—if the muscles and blood vessels of the extremities can by any means be stimulated equally as by walking, and the viscera receive concussion equal to that produced by the jolting of a horse, then all the purposes of exercise are accomplished; circulation is promoted; health is preserved; and a fair prospect of longevity is placed in full view.

"The means adapted to these ends,—the means of promoting circulation, and of preserving (restoring?) health to the diseased, the infirm, and the aged, are percussion and compression, (and more particularly friction). By the former (and by friction), the circulation is promoted, not only in parts affected with disease, but in the whole body. By the latter, vessels weakened by age or by disease are supported. This is not a speculative opinion, which may be right or wrong. It can be put to the test of experience by man, woman, or child, and its truth appreciated in five minutes. If a person sits in a cold room till his feet and legs become cold and benumbed, and a chilliness pervades the whole surface of the body, the application of percussion (or of friction, sufficiently long continued) will produce a glow of warmth over all the parts, equal to that produced by walking. When the blood has been repelled by cold from the surface of the body to the internal parts, it can be brought back again to the surface by percussion (and by friction). For wherever a stimulus is applied, to that part there is an afflux of blood; so that the equability of the circulation may be preserved in the sedentary, the diseased, the infirm, and the aged, in a degree highly conducive to health and longevity.

"When a person is attacked with rheumatism or gout, means are used to moderate the inflammation or fever, if present; and this being done, the patient is left to his fate. He may recover the use of his limbs, or he may never recover the use of his limbs; his medical adviser prescribes nothing but *patience and flannel*, which any other person could prescribe as well as he. Nay, the majority of medical practitioners do not hesitate to denominate any one as an impostor who would even propose to do anything further for the relief of a patient rendered perfectly lame from rheumatism or gout. The belief that has prevailed of rheumatism and gout being incurable, has superseded all endeavours to find out a cure. But these diseases may be prevented and cured as well as any other diseases. Nature herself teaches us the mode; for when seized with violent pain, we instinctively apply the hand to the part, and compress it (and rub it). Why, then, should we not follow nature's dictates, and improve her hints? When a person is first attacked with rheumatism or gout, a very slight manual operation would in the majority of cases prevent swelling, pain, rigidity of the extremities, and permanent lameness. Even where these diseases have, as it were, fixed their residence, the patient may have the perfect use of his limb restored, and be enabled thereby to take that exercise without which health must be imperfect and old age premature. Medical practitioners, however, encourage their patients in giving perfect rest to parts affected with rheumatism and gout, till, as often happens in the latter disease, the vessels change their action altogether, and secrete uric acid—a function they certainly never were intended to perform. It is incumbent on such practitioners to show that there is greater security to life in painful, rigid, and swollen limbs, and in frequent and long confinement, than in the free and equable circulation of the blood through

G

every part of the body, and in exercise in the open air.
It is incumbent on them to show that life is more
secure when the functions of the body are imperfectly,
than when duly performed. In other words, it is
incumbent on them to show that disease is preferable
to health, and more conducive to longevity. There is
not a sense or organ in the human body whose functions
are not preserved and improved by exercise. No wonder,
then, that so many rheumatic and gouty patients lose
entirely the use of their extremities."

After a few observations which do not strictly belong
to the subject, Dr. Balfour continues:—"Percussion
and compression (and friction) have been objected to in
gout on the score of their repelling the disease from the
extremities to vital organs. The objection has no
foundation whatever, either in matter of fact or in the
nature of things. I have cured lameness from gout in
innumerable instances, without any other consequences
than the patients being enabled to take that degree of
exercise which quickly restored them to perfect health.
It cannot be otherwise. Percussion (and friction),
instead of repelling, creates an afflux both of nervous
energy and sanguineous fluid to the part. Vessels in
a state of atony are thereby roused to action, and
circulation is promoted; and bandages support the
vessels, and enable them to perform their functions.
Where fever is present, I treat it on general principles.
But it is well known that the cure of rheumatism and
gout is not completed when fever is subdued—that
both these diseases often assume a chronic form, and
are not to be removed by the power of medicine."
* * * "Whoever has the slightest acquaintance
with natural philosophy and chemistry knows that
percussion produces wonderful effects on inanimate

bodies. A mason will cut a stone of immense thickness perpendicularly through by a few strokes of a hammer. A few strokes of a hammer will drive home a nail on which an immense weight, gradually applied, would have little or no effect. A smith's anvil may be made hot by continued and forcible hammering. Is it surprising, then, that a power which produces such wonderful effects on inanimate matter, should exert a powerful influence on the living body? If I apply percussion in the course of the sciatic nerve of a person labouring under sciatic rheumatism, a pleasurable vibration will be communicated through the whole limb, the nervous power being thereby diffused. If I apply percussion to a paralytic limb, I thereby attract to it the nervous energy. If I apply percussion to limbs debilitated by rheumatism, gout, or old age, I thereby excite the action of the vessels and nerves, promote circulation, and restore that heat of which they are deprived through inactivity and the weakness of the powers of life."

The major part of Dr. Balfour's book is occupied with the narrative of cases, of which I subjoin those that were treated by friction, in a very condensed outline:—

Case x.

Pain; weakness; rigidity of left hand, wrist, and fingers; effusion into the palm of the hand, and along the tendons of the fingers. Bandages and frictions. Cured in six days. The affection was of old standing.

Case xii.

In April, 1814, a lady was attacked by rheumatism in the shoulders, and afterwards in the knees. On May

2nd, 1815, the legs were permanently fixed in a slightly bent posture, and reduced to skin and bone. She could not rise, nor sit down, nor when sitting, raise her feet, especially from the floor. When she put them on a footstool, it was by grasping each leg with both hands a little above the knee, and lifting it up. It was impossible to make her stand, even when supported; for her limbs were entirely passive, and refused to do their office. When, therefore, she was lifted up for the purpose of being set upon her feet, she lay backwards in the arms of her assistant in a posture between the erect and horizontal. And when attempts were made to bring the trunk of the body to a line with the extremities, her feet moved, or were rather pushed forwards before her, for she possessed not the power of setting one foot before the other. Bandages, friction, and percussion restored her walking power in five months.

Case xiii.

In August, 1814, a young lady sprained her left knee. After various treatment, Dr. Balfour saw her on May 11th, 1815. There was inflammation of the joint, swelling, effusion, and excessive tenderness. The limb was permanently, but slightly, bent, and possessed a very slight range of flexion and extension. Bandages, friction, and percussion were employed, and her recovery was complete in July, 1815.

Case xiv.

May 15th, 1815. Madame Rey de la Ruaz. A general chronic rheumatic affection. All the fingers were extremely weak; some of them swelled, others so exquisitely painful that she could not suffer them to be touched. At Dr. Balfour's first visit, he touched by accident the point of her right thumb, which almost occasioned fainting. She could not lift a wine-glass with one hand, but she contrived to do it with both, by turning the backs to each other. Both wrist-joints were stiff and painful, but the left could not be moved without the greatest suffering. Both elbow-joints were greatly affected. The left did not possess half the natural range of flexion and extension. On each humerus, immediately above the inner condyle, a large tumour was situated, so painful that it could not be touched without making the patient cry out. All the muscles covering the humeri were, from origin to insertion, rigid, knotted, and thickened. The deltoid muscles felt like two boards. The connexion of the clavicles with the shoulders, and the joints at their flexures the patient could not suffer to be touched. She could not lift a hand to her head. At the under and back part of the right shoulder-blade, there was an extremely painful tumour, that prevented all motion of that bone; and a little farther down on the opposite side was another, still larger. From these tumours pains shot along both sides of the spine to the muscles of the back, rendering motion of it and of all the intermediate and neighbouring parts extremely difficult. At the top of each haunch-bone there was a large, painful tumour. Particular points of the sacrum and its connexions, especially with the coccyx, were so tender that they could not be handled but in the most cautious and delicate manner. The weight of a finger, rashly applied, occasioned the most excruciating torture. All about the hip-joints and great trochanters, as also the origins of the muscles of the thigh, were extremely painful. The muscles themselves were, through their whole course, tender to the touch, and painful on being compressed. On the outside of each thigh, a little above the knee-joint, there was a tumour of considerable size and extremely painful. The fascia of the muscles and sheaths of the tendons were thickened, knotty, and puffy. The flexor muscles were so contracted that their tendons were to the joints as the string is to the bow; the coverings of the joints themselves were thickened, puffy, and extremely tender; the range of flexion and extension of course very small. Such was Madame Rey's state when Dr. Balfour first saw her. Her head and a small part of the anterior of the trunk of her body were the only parts free from disease; *and she had not walked a step for eight years.* Friction, percussion, and bandages effected a cure, and enabled her to use her hands and arms, as in throwing a shawl round herself, in clasping her hands behind her neck, and in sewing for hours. She also regained her walking power.

Case xvi.

June 9th, 1815. J. C., Esq., Perth, aged 70. This was a case of very severe general chronic rheumatism. Sensible alleviation in a week by friction and percussion.

Case xvii.

Elizabeth Mackenzie, aged 20, seized in the winter of 1814—1815, with rheumatic affections of her feet and legs, that deprived her of their use for four months. In June, she walked with as much difficulty as it is possible to conceive of any human being at all capable of locomotion. Friction, percussion, and bandages effected a perfect cure.

Case xxi.

Mr. G., aged 80. July 11th, 1815. Injury to the parts surrounding the hip-joint and muscles arising from the pubes; from a fall. Consequent inability to walk except with the aid of crutches; partial lameness of arm, from injury to the shoulder. Rapid cure by friction and percussion, after four months' illness.

Case xxiii.

James Morison, aged 25. Rheumatic inflammation, with great effusion in left knee; pain in shin; rheumatism in left ankle; right shoulder and neck very painful. After five months of exquisite pain, and that everything at all likely to give relief had been tried in vain, a cure was effected by friction, percussion, and bandages, in a few weeks.

Case xxiv.

September 16th, 1815. Mrs. Mc C., of C., aged 60. Afflicted for three years and a half with rheumatism to a great degree. Dr. Balfour stayed three days, and performed five operations. Friction, percussion, and bandaging were employed; after which, she could put both her hands to the crown of her head with great boldness (which had been previously impossible); the pain in both deltoid muscles was gone. A tumour above the elbow-joints, and a chronic pain in this situation, had disappeared; both arms were more extended; the rotatory motion of both fore-arms was greatly increased; and the swelling of both wrists, and of the joints of the fingers, had visibly decreased. The pains were removed from both arms.

Case xxv.

John Macvean, aged 30. October 3rd, 1814. A case of acute rheumatism. Pains and inflammation of different parts were cured by friction, percussion, and bandages, in four days.

Case xxvi.

John Charles Thurso, aged 29. November, 1815. Had been ill two years. Pains in hip; could not raise his foot from the ground, but trailed it after him; ankle-joint painful and stiff; whole limb subject, when the foot was raised from the ground, to violent tremors, with spasms of the tibialis anticus tendon, which prevented entirely the motion of the joint. In six days, friction, percussion, and bandages removed these symptoms to a great extent.

Case xxix.

November 2nd, 1815. Sir T. T. Rheumatic pains of the hip and thigh, and loins and shoulder. Rheumatic inflammation of the ankle, with consequent lameness. Had been ill seven months, and had spent, without relief, five months at a watering place, and also had taken warm baths and tonics, with no good result. Friction, percussion, and bandages effected a cure in a month.

Case xxx.

November 6th, 1815. Lord M. Stiffness, rigidity, and pain of the muscles of the neck, completely preventing rotatory motion of the head. Cured by friction and percussion. Dr. Balfour draws attention to the immense discharges of flatus produced by his treatment of this case, and to the great improvement of digestive power which resulted.

Case xxxi.

November 22nd, 1815. Robert Anderson, aged 29. Rheumatism, of three and a half years' standing. The left arm possessed sufficient strength, but, the fingers excepted, had been of no more use to him for twelve months than a poker curved at one end and hung to his shoulder. This was owing to the elbow-joint being immoveably fixed with the arm in the extended state. The right arm was also as useless as a rod of iron suspended from the shoulder. The patient could not even, when sitting, lift his hand to his knee. When he wished to do this, he leaned backwards and threw it up by the shoulder, in the same way as he would have done had the limb been paralytic. The pain of the shoulder, elbow, and wrist was nevertheless excruciating. The rotatory motion of both fore-arms was not one-third of their natural range. When I asked this young man how he took his victuals, his reply was, "They are set for me at a certain height, and I am necessitated to take them just like a dog." Friction, percussion, and bandages produced in six weeks great improvement. He gained so much motion as to be able to eat like other persons, and Dr. Balfour considered that with perseverance a perfect cure would be effected.

"CODE OF HEALTH AND LONGEVITY."

"An Account of the Means by which Admiral Henry, of Rolvenden, in Kent, has cured Rheumatism, a tendency to Gout, the Tic Douloureux, the Cramp, and other Disorders; and by which a Cataract in the eye was removed; with Engravings of the Instruments made use of in the several operations practised by him."

It is well known that various modes of friction, or operating on the skin and muscles, are practised in different countries. In Europe the outside of the skin is rubbed with a flesh-brush, or with gloves made of hair or coarse woollen yarn; sometimes accompanied by fumigations. In the East Indies friction with the hand, or what is called shampooing, is well known; and the skin and muscles are pinched in order to render them pliable by the finger of the operator. A similar plan was likewise practised by Mr. Grosvenor, of Oxford; and Mr. Balfour, of Edinburgh has introduced with much success his system of compression. The operations practised by Admiral Henry, however, are still more extraordinary. But though the remedies were violent *(and hence not calculated for persons with inflammatory habits)*, yet they are not on that account to be rejected, and will in several respects stand a comparison with any system hitherto recommended. Cornaro, for instance, contrived, by the greatest privations, to preserve a vegetable kind of existence, by means of which, however, he could never have cured

himself of any of those violent disorders with which
the Admiral has been afflicted. Whereas the latter
was able to live without an unceasing attention to his
diet or mode of life, full of activity and spirit; and I
found him at the age of 91 in possession of his most
important faculties.

Admiral Henry was born at Holyhead, in the island
of Anglesea, on the 28th of September, 1731; and
consequently was on the 28th of September, 1823,
turned of 91. He went into the Navy in the year
1744. Whilst on service he had his thigh-bone broken
by a hawser in 1746. He was at the capture of the
Havannah in 1762, first lieutenant of the *Hampton
Court.* During the American War, in 1779, in consequence of his success in taking Mud Island in the
Delaware, which was considered at the time a most
important service, he was promoted to the rank of
captain by that distinguished admiral Lord Howe.
He was made an admiral in 1794; and in 1823 was
Admiral of the Red, and twelfth on the list. He was
married, but had no family.

Soon after the close of the American war, anno 1786,
Admiral Henry returned to the parish of Rolvenden,
in Kent, where he had formerly resided, and where
during his absence a house had been built for him in
the neighbourhood of a pleasant village about fifty-five
miles from London, twenty-one from Maidstone, and
three from Tenterden; where he continued to reside
with the exception of about a year and a quarter,
during which period he was on service with the late
Earl St. Vincent, and assisted in capturing the French
Islands in 1793 and 1794.

It was in the year 1787, however, that he began his
remedial operations on his body, and those only in a

very slight and trifling manner, not knowing but that
they might prove injurious, and his friends being
extremely apprehensive that he would do himself
much mischief.   But being of a persevering turn of
mind, and finding himself rather benefited than otherwise, he resolved to give the plan a fair trial.

Admiral Henry's system seems to be founded on the
following principles: 1,—That the chief cause of
disease in the human frame is deficiency of circulation;
and that the best means of correcting a tendency to
disease is to prevent the nerves and tendons from
falling asleep or getting fixed; for which purpose they
should be kept quite loose by instruments worked
among them; and 2nd,—That by keeping the blood-
vessels, nerves, and tendons in constant action, by
means of the bone instruments, the blood is rendered
pure; it passes quickly through the blood-vessels,
leaving no fur behind it; so that ossification, which
so frequently terminates the human existence, is
prevented.

In detailing the information communicated by
Admiral Henry, regarding the practices he has
adopted, it is proposed to explain,—

1st. *The Instruments used.*—The form of these
instruments will be seen in the frontispiece to this
volume.   They were at first made of bits of wood, as
they could easily be fashioned in any shape; but
finding that this material excoriated the skin, he was
induced to try bone, which answers better.   The bones
are boiled to take out grease, and then are smoothed
and shaped by a file.   The bone instruments are
principally made from the ribs of cattle; and it is a
great advantage to have them bent, as they can thus
be applied more successfully to the different parts of

the body. Any knobs are preserved; and others, where necessary, made with a file, so as to apply with effect across the tendons; as they are of great use in forwarding the process, particularly when situated in the middle of the bone. A list of the instruments is shown in the frontispiece, and shall afterwards be given.

2nd. *The Mode of Application.*—Every part of the body ought to be daily acted upon by some of these instruments, for the purpose of preserving health and warding off the infirmities of old age. It was in the year 1787 that he was accidentally led to apply the wooden tools to his knees, ancles, and insteps, which were all much swelled and hard, owing to the rheumatism, and very painful when touched; and though the operation was slightly done, yet he found considerable benefit from it. This gave him more confidence in the success of his plan, and induced him afterwards to try larger and stronger instruments, and to apply them with more force. To strengthen the feet, Admiral Henry was accustomed to tread the one over the other with the shoes off; and he also used the hammer, with a piece of cork, covered by leather at the end of it, for the soles; and the bone instruments to move the tendons. His feet thus became perfectly sound and well. By the same instruments, he greatly strengthened his heels, and the tendon achillis, both of which require constant beating, the circulation being very sluggish in both places. The thighs cannot be too much hammered, and if it is left off, they soon feel the want of it. The Admiral uses the round ends of common glass vials for that purpose, corked to prevent their breaking, and smoothed by a file. A solid piece of glass may likewise be used, made in the shape of a vial smooth at one end; the other should have a lip

like the common vial, but stronger and rounded, as it
then may be applied to move the tendons.

The Admiral's stomach and bowels had long been in
a very bad state; hard, painful when touched, and often
disordered; but by working them in bed with a bone
rounded at the end in each hand, digging into the
stomach as much as possible, particularly about the
navel, and making the two instruments meet among
the bowels, as much as they could be forced to, the
stomach is thus rendered so strong that it will digest
anything.* The whole of the breast should be worked
hard with the vials, and up and down over the lower
edge of the breast-bones. The collar-bone should be
treated in the same manner; and the bone instruments
should be also applied to the tendons under the cheek-
bones. The ends of the two thumbs should be applied
to each side of the gullet, and the gullet parted from
side to side with much force; which will prevent an
ossification of the throat, and keep the two passages
clear.

The mouth in general, and under the tongue, ought
to be treated in the same manner, either with the back
of a dessert silver spoon, or with tools made from the
handles of old tooth-brushes. The roof of the mouth
also should be thus rubbed, which prevents the swelling
of the uvula, and sore throats. The whole skin of the
head, more especially the hind part, requires to be
frequently rubbed and scraped by the bone instrument,
or by a table-spoon. It cleans off all scurf, and so
hardens the head that Admiral Henry, who before he
used these operations could not sleep without two

---

* The scrotum ought not to be neglected. It is singular that the
testes, which from age had become small, became in consequence of
those operations as large as ever they had been.

double flannel nightcaps, latterly wore only a single linen one in the coldest weather. The arms and hands are to be treated in the same manner, and with as much force as they can possibly bear. When he first applied the wooden instruments to the arms with great violence, he found that the flesh became discoloured, and he was obliged to desist for a fortnight; at the end of that period, however, he was enabled to apply the instruments again, without so much pain, and with benefit; when no pinching or blows discoloured the skin. Whenever he felt any part painful on the tools or instruments being applied to it, he was convinced that the nerves or tendons were diseased, and he never ceased working with the tools until there was no pain on their application, and the tendons felt loose.

Admiral Henry describes many of these operations as at first painful; but they cease to be so, if persevered in, and become even pleasant, and so useful that after going through them in the morning, one feels better all the day after. If regularly done for some time, the muscles become so sound and firm that neither pinching nor even beating with violence gives any pain; while with the improvement of the frame the mind becomes stronger, the spirits improve, and the faculties are strengthened.

3. *Cure of the Rheumatism.*—Admiral Henry was first affected with rheumatism in the year 1782, when he had it in so violent a degree that he could only crawl about, and at last became quite a cripple. Though he found himself much the better for the applications he had tried of wooden tools in 1787, yet the swellings in his knees, ankles, and insteps continued till the year 1810, when he began to use a common hammer made of iron with a bit of cork on the

head, and covered with leather. He persevered in
using this instrument for about three years, night and
morning, together with small bone instruments with
knobs, for loosening the tendons. He completely
succeeded in removing the swellings, and by keeping
up the practice was restored to the use of his limbs.

4. *Cure of Gouty Affections.*—Any tendency to the
gout felt by Admiral Henry was in the hand, and
particularly in the fingers, which became swelled and
contracted. The middle finger in particular had become
so extremely stiff that it was impossible to move it.
It bent upwards at the middle joint; the fore-finger
was also stiff. All these contractions and weaknesses,
by the use of the instruments, were completely
removed; and not only were the hands and arms
rendered firm and steady, but the fingers became
quite flexible.

5. *Cure of a Cataract.*—This most unpleasant complaint began to form on Admiral Henry's left eye in
the year 1782; but was neglected, as he saw well with
the right eye. He was accidentally led to rub it with
the eyelids closed, with the joint of the thumb, and
thought the eye was the better of it. He then began,
in hopes of dispersing the cataract, to use the round end
of a glass vial smoothed by a file. Sometime after he
perceived a glimmering of light; and being of a persevering disposition, continued the practice; and in less
than two years more the cataract was dispersed. About
two years afterwards a cataract came upon the right
eye, which gradually increased. He did not try the
friction plan with it; but was prevailed upon to get it
extracted as a quicker mode of cure. The operation
was performed with great skill by a distinguished
oculist in 1799, but an inflammation taking place, the

eye was lost; so that had it not been for the successful dispersion of the cataract in the left eye, the Admiral would have been quite blind.

6. *Cure of the Tic Doloureux.*—Admiral Henry remained for six weeks in London after the operation for the cataract, in hopes of something being done for his right eye; but in vain. He then returned to Rolvenden, and in about two months afterwards was seized with tic doloureux in that eye. Different washes were recommended to him, but though the directions were carefully attended to, they were of no use. This complaint continued for twelve months; he had two fits a day, of three or four hours each in duration, the eyes close shut the whole time, accompanied by the most excruciating torture. Hemlock, in great quantities, was then recommended, and a seton introduced behind the neck. By these means he was slowly relieved for about six months, but he was reduced to a state of great weakness. The complaint having ceased, the Admiral was advised to give up the hemlock and to heal the seton. In about a fortnight after, the pain returned with as much force as ever; and from his having been so much weakened, it became more severe. He then expected that it would destroy him. He accidentally was led to scrape the upper eyelid down for a few moments with a small piece of silver, which completely removed the complaint. He then conjectured that the nerve in which the pain was seated resides in that spot, for the operation of scraping had been tried on the temple and all round the eye, and was of no use. He continued to scrape the upper eyelid with the bone instruments.

7. *Cure of other Disorders.*—By the same operations other complaints are cured. Admiral Henry had

formerly been much troubled with corns, but had none
after he adopted the practice above described. It is an
effectual remedy against chilblains, to beat the heels
and feet with a broad wooden instrument, an engraving
of which is given. After speaking of the virtues of a
mixture of oil and rum for cuts and sore throats,
Sir John proceeds thus:—"With a common vial in
each hand, filed smooth at the end, Admiral Henry, by
pinching the legs from the heel to the ham very hard,
and the back, and inside of the thighs, has entirely
driven away the cramp."

8. *Miscellaneous particulars.*—In regard to diet,
Admiral Henry took anything that was presented to
him at breakfast or dinner, but no tea or coffee in the
evening, as it prevented his sleeping. For supper he
took boiled milk, with a large slice of stale bread either
boiled with it or put in afterwards, which is converted
into a kind of mucilage; and the same mess for
breakfast, when alone. He used no salt, pepper,
mustard, or vinegar, as he required no stimulant to
assist his digestion. He took at the rate of half-a-dozen
glasses of wine, either white or red, sometimes more
and sometimes less, unmixed with water, but as much
water afterwards as the wine he had taken, which
prevented any bad effects from the wine. In regard to
the alvine discharge, he was not regular; sometimes
once a day, sometimes every second or third day, and
sometimes once a week, which he considers as quite
sufficient. The fæces were always hard. He had
always at hand a bottle in which four ounces of Epsom
salts were dissolved in a quart of cold water; and if
costive longer than a week, he took a wineglass of this
medicine in bed at six in the morning, which carried
off all crudities. In regard to exercise, he was con-

stantly in motion, and never sat down, except when reading or at meals. The use of the tools which ensures the free circulation of the blood, renders any other sort of exercise less necessary. It may be proper to remark that the moderate, but persevering, use of dumb bells is of use in preventing the stooping of old age, which is owing to the muscles becoming relaxed, and thence the shoulders shrink and droop. There was nothing particular in his mode of clothing, except that he wore in cold weather, even in the house, a surtout of the common woollen stuff used for women's gowns, which cost him 20*d.* a yard. This dress in walking is very light; it was made to button its full length to below the knee. It thus keeps the wind off the body, and, not fitting close, always contains a warm atmosphere round the body. He never wore a cloth great coat, which, as it gets wet in rainy weather, he thought must be extremely injurious. As to sleep, he went to bed at nine o'clock when he had no company staying with him, and used his instruments in bed for a couple of hours. He seldom slept above from four to six hours, and if by accident he took more repose, he did not feel so well afterwards. He always got up with pleasure in the morning. Thus it appears that Admiral Henry, *with a view of preventing and curing disease*, took more liberty with the human frame than probably any man before him ever attempted. The result was, that Admiral Henry, at the age of above 91, had all the activity of middle age,—had got the better of several disorders with which he was afflicted, and attained as good a state of health as any man in England. In a communication dated 1st March, 1823, he thus describes his state :—" I never was better, and at present likely to continue so. I step up and down stairs with an ease which surprises myself. As to gout and similar complaints, they dare not approach. I have gone through every disorder that man can go through, but plague and fevers; and here I am in very good condition. I eat and drink most heartily; my digestion is excellent, and every food agrees. I can walk three miles to Tenterden without stopping."

Description of the Instruments.

1.—The hammer. It is covered with leather, and has a piece of cork at its head.

2.—An instrument made of wood, for beating the heels and soles, where the circulation is very sluggish. This prevents chilblains.

3.—The beater to be used in bed. It is short and handy for that purpose. To give it more force, it has some lead around the middle part of it, covered with leather.

4.—Bone instruments for rubbing various parts of the body, with knobs to work among the tendons.

5.—Small bone instruments for the inside of the mouth.

N.B.—The bones principally made use of by Admiral Henry are the ribs of cattle, boiled to take out the grease, and then smoothed and shaped by a file. Rib bones are naturally bent, which is a great advantage, as they can thus be more successfully applied to the different parts of the body. Any knobs are preserved, and others, where necessary, are made with a file, so as to be applied across the tendons, as they are of great use in forwarding the process, more especially if the knobs are situated near the middle of the bone.

DR. RAYNER.

In 1862, Dr. T. Rayner published a pamphlet of fifteen pages, entitled, "Practical Remarks upon the Treatment of various diseased states by Manipulation." Malvern, H. Cross. Price 3*d*.

This pamphlet, like that of Mr. Beveridge, Jun., contains no cases. It explains the views held by Dr. Rayner, as to the modus operandi of friction, and enumerates the affections in which he believes it to be useful.

In reference to the modus operandi of friction, Dr. Rayner says:—"The fact that impurities are present in the blood in most cases of disease, is now universally admitted, and it is well known that one of the most common results of a depraved condition of that fluid, consists in exudation or deposit of its morbid materials into the tissues or organs of the body. Among the organs which are frequently the seat of these exudations may be enumerated the muscles and nerves, with their sheaths, the tendons, and the fibrous expansions around the vertebræ and joints of the limbs. These deposits separate from the blood by exuding through the walls of the minute blood-vessels or capillaries in a liquid form, holding in solution various organic and inorganic matters, which unless speedily re-absorbed into the blood, solidify in the interstices of the tissues, or harden into masses or

layers, interfering with the circulation and function of
the part, producing stiffness by their bulk, and pain by
their pressure upon the nerves with which they are
in contact.

"These hardened deposits are more frequently present in chronic disease than is generally supposed; and
although the blood disease which originated them may
have been rectified by constitutional treatment (the
only manner in which this object can be attained), the
deposits it had previously produced are often only
capable of removal by firm, prolonged, and well-applied
friction, which mechanically softens and liquifies them,
and at the same time excites the activity of the
absorbents and blood-vessels, through which they pass
back into the blood, where they are oxygenized, during
respiration, into products capable of being eliminated
by the organs of excretion."

Again, p. 10, Dr. Rayner says:—"From what pre-
cedes, it will be seen that friction produces its curative
effects in several ways. First, as we have already
remarked, by softening and rendering soluble hard
deposits. Second, by exciting the activity of the
vessels, which absorb the dissolved materials into the
blood, in order that they may be carried out of the
body. Third, it acts as a counter-irritant, and with-
drawer of the excess of blood which oppresses congested
internal organs into the vessels of the muscles and skin,
thus restoring the balance of the circulation. Fourth,
it acts upon internal organs by sympathy, that is,
through the nerves which connect the external surface
with those organs whose torpid condition it is capable
of powerfully modifying. Fifth, there is no doubt
that friction acts mesmerically, or in other words that a
portion of the nervous force of the operator passes into

the bodies of those patients who are susceptible to its influence, especially when dry rubbing is practised."

The diseases which Dr. Rayner enumerates as likely to be benefited by friction are :—

1.—Sciatica, lumbago, and other forms of rheumatic and gouty neuralgia.

2.—Recent rheumatic inflammation of joints, when active inflammation has subsided.

3.—Congestion of the liver.

4.—Passive congestion of the brain and spinal chord.

5.—Paralysis, from congestion of the spinal chord and its membranes.

6.—In constipation, from want of nervous influence, he thinks that rubbing of the spine will be useful; and in constipation from want of contractile power in the lower bowel, he advises friction of the bowel itself.

7.—"As a substitute for active exercise, friction is invaluable."

8.—Clergyman's sore throat and throat deafness.

9.—Sprains and bruises, after inflammation has disappeared.

10.—Tuberculous deposits in glands and joints.

For the enlarged mesenteric glands of scrofulous children, Dr. Rayner recommends friction of the abdomen with cod-liver oil. And in pulmonary consumption he recommends friction of the chest with the same remedy.

APPENDIX.—II.

CASES TREATED BY MYSELF.

Case i.

RHEUMATIC GOUT.

MRS. COL. KITCHENER.

The lady whose case is described in the subjoined letter from her husband, was suffering, when she first saw me, from chronic inflammation of the hands, wrists, ankles, and feet. These parts were extremely deformed by gouty rheumatic effusions, which had so stiffened and wasted them that they more resembled wooden than fleshy limbs. She could just hobble a yard or two, but not without consequent pain and increase of inflammation in the ankles. She could not sew, play the piano, nor use her hands in any way. She was also in very poor condition, having been kept for a year on fish diet, with the frequent use of purgatives. Moderate water treatment, however, so restored her general health, that she gained more than a stone in weight, while the local frictions, diligently and daily applied, gave her back the power of walking, and of using her hands in knitting, playing the piano, &c. The inflammation was entirely cured, but it was found to be impossible to bring back the wrists, fingers, &c., to their *healthy* pliability, as the disease had made too great ravages when she came to me. However, she gained immense benefit, as her husband's letter will testify:—

" May 18th, 1857.

" My dear Dr. JOHNSON,

    "I have put off writing to you for some time, feeling that it would be satisfactory to you to know that the improvement my wife gained whilst with you at Malvern is permanent. I am happy to say that at the end of a month I see no return of the disease. She is gaining strength. I feel it a duty to you, and to others who may be similarly situated, to state the facts of her case. Four years ago, Mrs. Kitchener was attacked with rheumatic gout, swellings, and weakness of her joints, and general debility. Local advice failed, after trying hot baths, colchicum, &c. She then took what we thought the best advice in Dublin, which sent her to Buxton. After going through the regular course of baths, under medical superintendence, and it producing but little good effect, I took her to London; and after consulting several medical men, placed her, by their advice, under the most eminent for that disease. Still no cure. I had made up my mind to break up my establishment, and seek for her health amongst the Continental Spas, when, providentially I may say, my friend, Capt. Anketell, visited me, and persuaded me to try the water cure for her (which I had been previously afraid of), upon his describing your kindness to your patients and gentleness of treatment. When she went to you, she was unable to walk, could hardly turn in bed, work, or play the piano. I need not tell you how much better she was before she left your establishment; but you will be pleased to know our friends here are quite astonished at her appearance, and to see her walking about and enjoying herself.   Indeed, I can hardly believe my eyes, when I see her, rake in hand, working in her garden, upon recollecting only a year ago an eminent medical man told me we could have no hope of her case being better, and all I could do was to enable her to bear it until it wore her out.   After stating what I have done, it is needless to say how grateful we feel to you for your constant care and judicious treatment during her seven months residence under your roof. Mrs. K. begs me to add that she considers her recovery very much assisted by Cameron's (the person who rubbed her) skill and attention.   She joins with me in kind regards, and I remain, faithfully yours,

"H. K. KITCHENER."

Case ii.

MISS ——————

CHRONIC INFLAMMATION OF THE KNEE-JOINT OF SEVEN YEARS STANDING, CURED IN ABOUT A YEAR.

Miss —— was brought to me in the winter of 1857, from Pau, where she had been staying two years, for the disease in her knee.   Seven years back, from an injury, inflammation attacked the ankle and knee of the right leg, and laid her up.   From that time to the time when she first saw me she had been unable to walk, as any exertion brought on increased inflammation, pain, swelling, &c.   She had enjoyed the advice of the most eminent surgeons of Edinburgh and London, but no one had succeeded in even checking the disease, before I saw her.   There was great enlargement of the knee-joint, so that its shape was quite indistinguishable. It was highly reddened from inflammation, and so tender that she could not bear the weight of the bed-clothes upon it. The joint was quite fixed and contracted and motionless, and the knee-pan could not be stirred. The leg was contracted at a right angle with the thigh, a most inconvenient form of contraction. The ankle was also inflamed, and full of synovial effusion, and *the foot was fixed in a right line with the leg.* It could not be bent back into its natural position on account of contraction of the ligaments. The whole leg was affected with interstitial effusions. The periosteum, cellular tissue, muscles, &c., being all hardened, lumpy, painful, and incapable of motion. A more hopeless case could not well be imagined, short of suppuration. It was what is commonly called a case of white swelling. In addition the left knee, leg, and ankle had, within the last year, begun to swell, and become knotted, with effusions, and painful, with more or less of inflammation; so that there was every reason to apprehend that the left leg was going to become as bad as the right.

This lady was put upon a course of frictional treatment, combined with some bathing; and in about a year she was perfectly cured.

The merit of this cure is due to the frictions; for the effect of the water treatment was only to improve the general health, and to alleviate the inflammation, which, however, did not disappear completely until the absorption of the morbid matters in and about the knee-joint was completed by the operation of the frictions. In the latter stage of treatment the douche proved very serviceable. In a letter received May 16, 1859, the lady says, after a few remarks which it is unnecessary to

quote, " It will give you unfeigned pleasure, I am sure,
to know that I am a great deal stronger than when I
wrote to you last. A looker-on could hardly discover
a very slight lameness that only comes on when the
day is done, and its work, and I am fatigued. The
more I walk the more I am able to walk, as you often
foretold me would be the case; and now I think
nothing of two hours' walking. My dear father, as you
may suppose, is most delighted. Yesterday we went
up the banks of the Findhorn (the beautiful river
which I think I spoke to you of), and we scrambled on
its banks for two hours, besides walking and a drive of
twenty-five miles. How can I ever thank you sufficiently for opening up such pleasures to me?" In a
letter received about two months later the lady states
that her recovery was then perfect, as she could walk,
ride, drive, do anything in short like other people,
without feeling inconvenience. There is now no vestige
of stiffness or contraction of any part. The case just
narrated made a great sensation in the lady's native
place, and a medical gentleman of the neighbourhood
having occasion to write to me concerning a patient
whom he had sent to me, remarked incidentally,
"Miss ——'s knee is the most wonderful cure I
ever knew."

Case iii.

LAMENESS, FROM MORBID DEPOSITS ABOUT THE BACK, HIPS, AND THIGHS.

Mrs. B., a middle-aged lady, three years ago caught
cold from exposure in snowy weather. From that
period she began to feel pain and stiffness in the right
leg, and to lose the power of walking. These symptoms

continually increased, notwithstanding the use of the
Buxton waters, and a visit to a German spa, and
other measures. In Germany, the limb was rubbed
a great deal (but after the manner of Mr. Grosvenor
and ordinary shampooers, with the flat hand), and the
douche was employed. In spite of the assiduous use of
these and similar remedies, when Mrs. B. came under
my treatment, nine weeks ago, she was quite unable to
walk. She could contrive to get along a few paces by
leaning on another person's arms, but not further,—
partly from pain and stiffness, and partly from the
want of power. She could get up a few stairs by
putting the left leg in the ordinary way upon the step
above, and then lifting the right leg after it; but she
could by no means walk up stairs in the usual manner.
Now, after nine weeks' rubbing, she can and does walk
a quarter of a mile without the assistance even of a
stick, and that four times in the day. She says she
considers her improvement "quite wonderful," and
that when she finds herself going about, she does not
know how to believe the fact. She can go up stairs
like other people. In this case, examination disclosed
a surprising number of very large lumps, distributed
all over the sacrum, hip, and thigh; some were as large
as an egg; some were very hard; others were softer.
They were chiefly seated in the areolar tissue; but some
implicated the muscles of the gluteal region, and those
about the neck of the femur and of the thigh. They
disappeared to a great extent under the processes
employed, and a number of boils and an eruption came
out on the leg. The limb, which had been generally
cold and pale, became warm, and the skin pink,
and the flesh assumed to the touch the softness
proper to health.

Case iv.

PARALYSIS OF LOWER EXTREMITIES, AND THICKENING
OF THE EXTERNAL TISSUES.

George Palmer, aged 36, railway porter at Weston-super-Mare and Bristol, was taken in February, 1856, with very severe pain in the back. In his own words, "When he was down, it prevented him getting up." Two days after, he was taken stiff in the right leg, and lost all power whatever over it. There was also great pain in the whole limb. He had besides pain in the head. Two medical men attended him, both of whom stated that he was suffering from paralysis, and they treated him thus:—They applied a blister over the buttocks and thighs for two days and nights, and a second blister over the exterior part of the thigh, from the ilium to the knee. He had blisters to his back, two or three blisters between the lower edge of the left ribs and the groin, a blister on each side of the knee, followed by blistering ointment, and four issues over the sciatic notch. In April, 1857, he had six leeches behind the ears to relieve pain in the head. During the whole of his illness, he was taking medicine continually. But neither blisters, nor issues, nor medicine did him a particle of good. Towards the latter part of June and in July he took, during four or five weeks, hot salt baths at Weston. These strengthened his nerves and general system, but failed to touch his paralysis. It was, I think, on July 28th, that I first saw him in Malvern, whither he had been sent by a benevolent lady, Mrs. Whiting, who desired to have my opinion upon his case. He was then perfectly paralysed in the right leg, retaining only very slight motion of the toes. He was incapable even of rising from bed, for all he could do was to roll himself over. He could not stand without assistance, and he could not walk. Examining his person minutely, I found much hardening and thickening about the sacrum, the sciatic nerve, and down the legs. I was led, therefore, to regard this as a case of peripheral or rheumatic paralysis, and to believe that a cure might be effected, if the indurations above described could be removed. In consequence, I undertook his treatment, and had him vigorously rubbed every day, and gave him a course of blanket sweatings. The result of all this was a complete, and indeed a surprising cure, as the following letter will testify:—

"*Somerset House, Great Malvern, Nov. 26th,* 1857.

"Dear Sir,—I beg to return my sincere and heartfelt thanks for your unwearied attention and great kindness to me since it has been my good fortune to know you. I certify that I was seized with paralysis of the spine and right leg, in Feb., 1856, and eighteen months from that time was under the treatment of two eminent allopathic doctors, from whom I derived no benefit. But providentially, by the benevolence of a lady, I was enabled to come to Malvern on the 28th of July, 1857, in a perfectly helpless state, and under your energy and skill, I can now walk eight to ten miles a day, without crutches or stick.

"I am, Sir,
"Your humble and most grateful servant,
"GEORGE PALMER.

"Dated this 26th day of November, 1857.

"Dr. Walter Johnson,
    Bury, Great Malvern."

On his restoration to health, I took George Palmer into my service as rubber, and for some years he served in that capacity, and never had the slightest symptom of a return of his old ailment, but always enjoyed robust health.

Case v.

PARALYSIS AND ATROPHY OF ARM, AFTER TYPHUS FEVER.

The annexed is the account which I received of Jane Jenkins, before she was placed under my care:—
"Jane Jenkins, nearly eighteen years of age, rather more than five years ago, had the typhus fever. When quite recovered, suddenly she lost the use of her left arm, which at the time became almost black, but now is the natural colour, excepting that it is a more deadly white. Previously to this, J. J. had suffered from acute pain at the back of the head, and does so now at intervals. Her health not generally strong, and a variable appetite. She was in the Chester Infirmary eight weeks, where a liniment was rubbed on the affected arm. No good result, though, seemed to follow. Galvanism was tried for a short time; and a little benefit J. J. thought she derived from it. The arm at times aches very much, especially near the shoulder. Until about a year ago, she could work a little with her needle, but now that has had to be given up. The arm is not entirely powerless; she can move it a little, but if she attempts to hold anything, it trembles very much. It is rather smaller than the other arm."

The impression which the appearance of this girl's arm produced is shown by a remark made by a person who saw it with me:—" It is like an arm dug out of a coffin, and cemented to her shoulder." Friction, regularly applied, produced, after a few months, a perfect cure; and Jane Jenkins was able to carry into execution what had been her dearest wish,—she went into the business of a dress-maker.

Case vi.

EFFECTS OF SPRAIN IN WRIST.

Miss ——, after a sprain, became the subject of inflammation of the wrist. The ordinary treatment having failed to do any good, she applied to me. The wrist was inflamed, swollen, red, painful on being touched, and the wrist-joint, as well as the sheaths of the flexor tendons, were full of fluid, of a thick character, which contained also grain-like concretions. The wrist was fixed. The fingers were fixed in a bent position; and the hand was consequently useless. Rubbing was used in this case very sedulously, and with a very happy result. The inflammation was removed, the wrist regained its mobility, and the fingers were released and made flexible. All that remained behind of the affection was a certain weakness of the wrist, which incapacitated the young lady from playing the piano and from performing similar actions which require a rather powerful and continued effort; but all the ordinary actions of common life were easily and effectually performed.

Case vii.

SCIATICA.

Miss R. had for a long time tried to get relief from a very painful chronic sciatica. She could not sleep for the restlessness and pain in the angry sciatic nerve. She had been treated by one allopathic and by two homœopathic medical gentlemen in succession, but without the least advantage. Rubbing, applied to the affected part, completely cured the disease in a few weeks.

[Sciatica is one of the diseases most amenable to friction. I have known many very striking cases of cure.]

Case viii.

NEURALGIA IN KNEE.

Mr. R. had tried in vain to get cured by ordinary means of a syphilitic inflammation, attended with neuralgic pain in the knee. The knee was rubbed in my establishment, and the swelling, pain, and inflammation were entirely removed.

Case ix.

HEADACHE.

Master W. was subject to chronic headaches. On examination, his neck was found to be extremely stiffened and hardened, and it was consequently rubbed. At the same time, he took water treatment, and was put upon a system of dieting. The neck, after a while, softened, and the headaches disappeared.

Headaches are frequently found to depend upon a thickened and hardened state of the neck and shoulders, and the removal of this morbid condition removes the headache.

Cases x. & xi.

ENLARGED GLANDS IN THE NECK.

Miss M. and Miss G. In these cases, enlarged glands in the neck were removed by friction. I merely mention these two cases in illustration of the power which rubbing has of causing the absorption of enlargements, whether glandular or other, as I have no notes of the cases.

Case xii.

ENLARGED GLANDS IN THE NECK.

Robert T., aged 16, came to me April 9th, 1866. Six months ago, he had typhus fever. He was confined to bed two weeks, and gradually got better, but is still far from well, having a brown tongue, bad appetite, feelings of weakness, &c. Three months ago, the glands in the neck began to swell, and have continued to swell to the present time. They are now greatly enlarged on the right side, and very hard. This patient was subjected to a course of water treatment, including Turkish baths, and the glands were rubbed one hour a day. On May 7th, he discontinued the treatment, and returned home. The glands were very remarkably reduced in size, and the general health was re-established.

Case xiii.

RHEUMATIC ANCHYLOSIS OF SHOULDER JOINT.

"*Edge Hill, Derby, Feb. 18th,* 1866.

"My dear Dr. JOHNSON,

"I have very much pleasure in sending, as you request, an account of the case of the young woman whom you so benevolently treated, and on whom you effected so marvellous a cure. It was about October, 1859, that Mary Ann Barker, the daughter of a bricklayer, aged about 27, came to me for an order of admission to the Derbyshire Infirmary. I observed that she made no use of her right arm, and on inquiry learnt that she was unable to bend it,—that she had suffered from rheumatic fever, for which she had been in the Infirmary two months, and left with her arm stiff, and was told it would always be so. I had her arm examined by a surgeon, who also communicated with the house surgeon, and the surgeon who attended her. He told me it was anchylosis of the joint, and that they attempted to break the covering of the joint, but had not succeeded; and added that her surgeon said, 'If Dr. Johnson could cure her arm, he could work a miracle.' I think it was about the beginning of November that I sent her to Malvern, and you most kindly attended to her till early in the following April, when you sent her back to Derby with her arm perfectly cured. She was able to move it in all directions without pain or difficulty; and I had her taught a trade in a silk factory, which required constant use of the arm to turn a wheel, and she was able to earn a good living, which, but for your skilful treatment, would have been quite impossible. I sent her to my friend the surgeon, who had seen the case before she went to you, and also to the one under whose care she had previously been, and who had said that 'only a miracle could cure her.' He admitted that it was extraordinary. I saw her frequently for a year or two after she came back, but have lost sight of her now for some time. Up to the last time I saw her, the arm continued all right. I think this is the best case of cure I have seen by friction, as you apply it. But I have seen many others, and some very extraordinary. My own was not a bad one. After suffering greatly from pain in the lower part of the back for seven years, and having undergone all sorts of treatment for neuralgia, affection of the lumbar nerves, &c., without any relief, I put myself under your care in 1857, and in a very short time I was quite well, and have had no return since, beyond an occasional twinge, which I thought it best to treat at once; and two or three days under your roof set me quite right. I am so thoroughly convinced of the value of your system of rubbing, that I have been happy to get several of my friends to place themselves under you, and always with benefit. I now enclose a letter from our friend Mrs. B., whom it took me four years' continual persuasion before I could get her to go to Malvern, and she is now most grateful, as her letter shows, both to you and to me. You are perfectly welcome to make any use you please of this letter; and I should be very happy to answer any inquiries on the subject from any one.

"Believe me always yours very truly,
"JOSIAH LEWIS."

Case xiv.

CHRONIC INFLAMMATION OF THE KNEE-JOINT.

Extract from a Letter from Mrs. B., to J. Lewis, Esq.

"And now, about our friend Dr. Johnson. I shall only be too happy to add my testimony to the efficacy of rubbing and water. He may put my initials in stating my case; and I shall be most glad to be referred to. Dr. Johnson knows my case when I first went to him. I had then been under medical treatment for two years,—mercurial strappings and various tortures in the way of instruments applied, all for the worse. Then came Malvern treatment; and though not a *cure*, wonderful effects, and every day improving. I can walk a mile and back, stand, and saunter about the greater part of the day; and before I went to Malvern I used to lie and sit, and *never* move or walk, save down stairs of a morning, up at night, and just to the table at meals; never putting my feet to the ground when I could help it. This is the simple outline.

Dr. Johnson must make it up as he pleases. And thanks, 10,000, to you for *plaguing* me into going."

I think it needless to comment upon the above case, further than to remark that it was a case of chronic inflammation of the knee-joint, and that I treated it by friction, with some water appliances. I expect a complete cure, unless in case of interruption by imprudence or accident.

Case xv.

LAMENESS FROM CHRONIC RHEUMATISM OF ANKLE-JOINTS.

"*Bewdley, Feb.* 19th, 1866.

" Dear Dr. Johnson,

"You are quite at liberty to publish the successful result in my case of your mode of treatment. I had suffered increasingly for two years from what my medical attendant pronounced chronic rheumatism in the joints; and I had become utterly unable to walk. After trying many other remedies under varied and eminent advice, I was induced to place myself under your care. I soon lost all acute symptoms of the disease, and within six months was again able to walk with ease and pleasure. I should confidently recommend any friend of mine similarly afflicted to adopt the same course of treatment; and I rejoice that you are about to make it more widely known by your proposed publication.—I am, yours sincerely,

"ELIZABETH MARCY."

In this case, the cure was effected by friction, which caused absorption of the fluid effused, chiefly in the ankles. When the ankle-joint is distended by an over-abundant secretion, lameness results, as in this case, and in a large number of cases no treatment is found to be effectual but appropriate rubbing.

Case xvi.

NEURALGIA IN THE NECK.

"*Feb.* 12*th*, 1866.

"*Newbold Rectory, Shipston-on-Stour.*

"Dear Dr. WALTER JOHNSON,

"You recollect how the water treatment made a new man of me years ago. Still, it did not remove what I had long before that treatment been suffering from, and what I supposed to be rheumatic pain in my neck and shoulder. I used to say it was as if a hot wire were being passed through the vertebræ of the neck. By your advice I put myself in the hands of the rubber. He soon discovered, under the pressure of his finger and thumb, numerous little knots, of callous substance, which he called 'grittle,' pressing upon the nerves and muscles, and quite enough to account for the pain, often excruciating, which I had long been suffering. As the parts became warm under his rubbing, the callous substances by degrees became soft; and then it was not long before they were rubbed clean away; and with the help of the baths, which I was taking daily at the time, soon disappeared. A very few weeks of the rubbing so far set me up that I was wonderfully relieved and comparatively comfortable. A repetition of it for a still shorter time, I think about a year later, quite completed the cure; and I am most thankful to say, I have had no return of the pain for the last two or three years, and am now entirely free from it. I am very glad indeed to hear you are going to publish a treatise on rubbing; and hoping it may add as much to the health and comfort of others as it has done to mine, I remain, with all good wishes,

"Gratefully and sincerely yours,

"RICHARD PRITCHARD."

In the chapter on the pathology of friction, I have dealt very sparingly in theories. I have preferred to give an exact description of the actual phenomena, and to leave to physiologists the task of harmonising them with general views of disease and cure. But since reading Dr. Handfield Jones's work on "Functional Nervous Disorders," and observing the large part which the theory of "Inhibition" plays in his system, I think I ought not to put forth this little Essay without making a few remarks on the application of that theory to the explanation of the effects of friction of the human body.

The fundamental facts on which the doctrine of "Inhibition" is based may be thus stated:—M. Bernard, the great French experimental physiologist, found that when the sympathetic nerve in the neck was divided, or the superior cervical ganglion extirpated, the following phenomena occurred:—"The temperature of the operated side increased rapidly, and in a quarter of an hour had risen 11° F.; the arteries and small vessels dilated, and became much more full of blood than those of the opposite side. The increased flow of blood, which is the immediate result of the operation, subsides considerably in a day or two. But the elevation of the temperature was much more persistent, lasting in rabbits sixteen or eighteen days; in dogs, six weeks to two months. Not only the superficial parts, but the deep-seated; and even the blood returning by the jugular vein can be shown to be hotter than the corresponding parts of the healthy side, or than they themselves were previously."

It is known that the coats of the blood-vessels are elastic, and that under varying influences they expand and contract, just as the hose of a fire engine may be seen to do when the engine is playing. The coats of the blood-vessels are covered with a fine net-work of nerves, united with and forming part of that great nervous chain which we call the sympathetic system; and this net-work of sympathetic filaments is termed the "vasomotor" nerves. Now, from M. Bernard's experiment above related, and from the result of others by other experimentalists, the following doctrine has been deduced:—It is thought that in the state of health the vasomotors convey to the blood-vessels from the sympathetic (and in some cases, perhaps, from the spinal) centres, an influence which has the effect of calling into action the elastic contractile fibres of the coats of the vessels. Hence, in health, the tonic, or semi-contracted, condition of the vessels. Excision of a sympathetic ganglion, or even a certain kind of stimulus of a ganglion, interrupts the passage of such influence; in other words, checks, stops, "inhibits" the action of the vasomotors. As an immediate consequence, the coats of the vessels, losing their elasticity, yield to the heart's driving force, and expand; a larger volume of blood flows into the tissues, and we have the phenomena above described—those of "congestion."

It is very possible that the effect of friction may be "inhibitional." It may act by breaking, in an intermittent manner, the vis nervosa current, which is said to flow from the sympathetic centres to the vasomotors distributed over the blood-vessels. If so, to every interruption of the current by the passage of the finger over a nerve will correspond a momentary dilatation of vessels, influx of blood, increase of heat, and other congestive phenomena. And a rythmical series of such interruptions will be followed by the permanent effects detailed in the body of this work.

FINIS.